THE
KING'S RIFLE

Also by Biyi Bandele

Fiction
The Street
The Sympathetic Undertaker and Other Dreams
The Man Who Came In From the Back Of Beyond

Plays
Brixton Stories
Happy Birthday, Mister Deka D
Me and the Boys
Death Catches the Hunter
Oronooko
Things Fall Apart
Thieves like Us
Yerma
Resurrections
Two Horsemen
Marching For Fausa
Señora Carrar's Rifles (*translation*)

Screenplays
The Kiss
Bad Boy Blues
Not Even God Is Wise Enough

THE
KING'S RIFLE

BIYI BANDELE

Previously published under the title *Burma Boy*

Amistad

An Imprint of HarperCollins*Publishers*

This book is dedicated to the 500,000 troops from the Royal West African Frontier Force and the King's African Rifles who served with the Allied Forces during the Second World War.

And to the memory of my father, Solomon 'Tommy Sparkle' Bamidele Thomas, a 'Burma Boy' whose stories of war in the jungle echo still in my ears.

And to my son, Korede, and my daughter, Temi.

Contents

The gun arrived, and I checked it, wondering how
much the men knew about the thing.

'Who's number one?'

'Me be,' exclaimed Private Ali Banana.

– James Shaw, The March Out.

PROLOGUE: CAIRO

1

Two years into the war, on a day so hot and stifling the usually bustling thoroughfares of Cairo were all but deserted, a spare, dishevelled looking Englishman with a stooping gait staggered through the city's dark alleyways and bazaars, jostling with horses, camels, bicycles, mopeds, pushcarts, pedestrians and cars, looking, he said, for a chemist. To every hawker he approached and tried to speak to, on narrow, congested streets wafting with the odour of ginger, cumin, sandalwood and mint; and at every shisha-pipe-smoke-filled coffee house he wandered into, it seemed, as he struggled to speak but seemed only to slur, that he was looking for something which existed only in his fever-sapped imagination; that much was clear, that this strange man, dressed in a British army uniform that hung loosely on his shrunken frame, and wearing a major's rank, was in the grips of a fierce and crippling fever. He shivered under the blistering heat, his teeth clattering as if he were in the deep chill of an English winter's day.

'Chemist,' he mouthed. 'Atabrine.' But the words came out in a meaningless slur. Clearly the man was ill. And yet his deep-set, pale blue eyes glared defiantly from a bony, thin face overgrown with a shaggy beard.

Curses and insults followed him as he staggered from one side of the street to the other without looking where he was going, and as he crossed the road back and back again without any apparent concern for his life or for oncoming traffic. A donkey-cart messenger who ended up in a sewage drain when he swerved to avoid the man ran after him and heartily wished divorce on his parents; a jitney driver who stepped on his brakes only just in time leaned out of his car and threatened, firstly, to impregnate the officer's mother, and secondly, to make a cuckold of him, and thirdly, to run him over next time. Then, in swift contrition, and asking God to forgive him for the sins of his mouth, the driver bundled the crazed British officer into his car and, having failed to draw out a lucid response when he asked where to take him, drove straight to the Continental Hotel in the city centre, which everyone knew was packed with Allied officers. There he palmed him off to the concierge, like an unwanted gift, and dashed back to his car, speeding off before the loathsome offering could be forced back on him. The driver need not have worried. He had brought Major Wingate back to the right place.

The concierge's face was creased with worry.

4

'Is the major all right?' he asked.

The major was far from all right. But the ride in the car seemed to have given him back his tongue. 'Take your filthy hands off me,' he snapped. 'I am not a cripple.'

The concierge winced and then bowed apologetically. 'Of course, Major Wingate,' he said. 'Forgive me, sir. I was only trying to assist.'

Wingate was shaking violently, as if he was having a spasm. 'The only help I need right now,' he quivered, 'is Atabrine. I must have Atabrine.'

'Atabrine,' said the concierge. He considered the word, mouthed it a few times, tried various ways of pronouncing it, paused thoughtfully and then shook his head. 'The name sounds familiar, sir,' he said gravely.

'What name?'

'Atabrine, sir. Is he one of our guests?'

The world spun around Wingate as he headed into the lobby. He went to the reception desk, ignoring an officer calling out to him from the crowded bar.

'Tayib, Tayib,' he said with obvious relief when he saw the receptionist, 'get me some Atabrine.'

'But Major Wingate,' Tayib beamed solicitously, 'I got you a whole bottle of Atabrine only yesterday.'

'All gone,' Wingate muttered.

'*All*, sir?' A line of sweat broke out on the receptionist's brow.

'I took the last two tablets this morning.'

'That was meant to last a week,' Tayib said gently.

Behind Wingate, at the bar across the lobby, the colonel was waving.

'Someone is trying to catch your attention, sir.'

'Get me another week's dosage, will you, Tayib?' He sounded desperate.

'Colonel Mitchell, sir, is trying to tell you something.'

Wingate turned and looked, with evident distaste, at the colonel. 'Ape,' he hissed before swinging round again to face Tayib. 'Well?' he said.

'Doctor Hamid —' Tayib began.

'Sod him.'

'Indeed, sir. But the prescription I got you yesterday came from Doctor Hamid, and Doctor Hamid left Cairo only this morning to visit his father in Alexandria.'

'I need Atabrine. I'm putting my trust in you, Tayib. I'll be in my room.'

'I'll see what I can do, Major Wingate.'

The receptionist watched Wingate struggle unsteadily towards the lift. Then he called out to the concierge, 'Ahmed.'

The concierge sauntered over to the front desk.

'I need some Atabrine,' Tayib said.

'What happened to the batch I picked up yesterday from Doctor Hamid?'

'Can you or can you not get me some from your brother-in-law?'

'Why can't you get it from Doctor Hamid?'

'Why must you always answer a question with a question?' Tayib leaned closer and said, 'I got quite an earful from him yesterday when I telephoned for the batch you picked up.'

'Doctor Hamid loves the sound of his own voice.

Especially when he's about to slap you with a heavy bill.'

'That wasn't the problem. The problem was that the major simply came to me and said, "Tayib, get me some Atabrine."'

'Naturally. He seems to think Atabrine grows on trees.'

'So I telephoned Doctor Hamid. And he said to me, "Where's the patient? Bring him here to my clinic," he said. "Tell him I want to see him."'

Atabrine was known to be toxic and unpredictable. Even when taken in the recommended dosage, the doctor explained to Tayib, it was sometimes impossible to tell its side-effects apart from the worst symptoms of the illness it was meant to cure. It had been known to induce a deep psychosis in some people and had sent others into a coma. It was crucial, Doctor Hamid said, to examine the patient before prescribing Atabrine. But Tayib knew that it was futile to go back to Wingate with such a message.

'So I said to him, "Doctor," I said, "I cannot bring Major Wingate to you. He's just spent the last year or so in Abyssinia fighting the Italians. There's a rumour something went badly wrong for him out there and he's lost his marbles."'

'That's no rumour.'

'"It's Atabrine or my job," I said to him. So he took pity on me and said to send someone along to pick up a week's dosage. "Next time, he said, remember I'm a physician, not a pharmacist."'

Down by the lift, Wingate was resting against the wall, shaking as he waited for the lift to come.

'Did you know that back in Abyssinia your major was a colonel?'

'No!'

'May I divorce if I tell a lie. And what happens the moment the Italians surrender? What happens after the Abyssinian war is over? He's ordered by his commanders to report immediately to GHQ Cairo. Why? Well, no one knows. But the first thing he got when he went to GHQ was news that he was now a major. A demotion. I don't know what crime he committed in Abyssinia but I hear he might even be facing a court martial. There's more to that man's haggard, wasted look than malaria. There's a cloud hanging over his head. And I for one feel no sympathy for him. He's the rudest, most uncouth guest I've ever encountered in all the years I've worked here. Did you see him on the day he checked in? He arrived chewing an onion. An onion, Tayib. Don't get me wrong, I do like onions. But an onion is not an apple. At first I thought it was an apple he was biting into so greedily. But it wasn't an apple. The man was eating a raw onion. You think you've seen everything, Tayib, and then you meet a creature like that. Vile. Vile.'

'How soon can you get to your brother-in-law?'

'My brother-in-law is a cheap, lying, fornicating quack.'

'That may be so, but I didn't ask for a description of your brother-in-law.'

'He's a slimy back-street abortionist.'

'The question is, does he have Atabrine?'

'I wouldn't go to him if I had a sore throat.'

'Do me this favour, Ahmed.'

The lift had arrived. As he went inside, Wingate missed a step and ended up on his knees. Tayib immediately reached for the phone. 'What that man needs isn't more Atabrine. He's had too much of that already. Go back to your post, Ahmed. This is no matter for a quack abortionist. I'm calling the Royal Army Medical Corps.'

'Why didn't he go to them in the first place?'

'If I could read minds, Ahmed, do you think I would be trapped behind this desk?'

He dialled the operator and asked for the RAMC.

In the lift, Wingate somewhat groggily tried to call his floor but his hands seemed to have gone into sudden revolt and every time he thought of a new task for them, no matter how basic, they simply hugged the wall tighter and refused to obey him. The ache in his head, just above his eyes, was like a migraine followed by a kick in the skull. He could barely see, and when he could see, the effort was so draining, so painful, he closed his eyes and prayed that he would pass out. Even with his eyes shut, he could see vividly the cut-glass chandeliers and electric lamps hanging down the ceiling of the lobby. They twinkled like countless stars and see-sawed dangerously – any minute now they would come hurtling down and crush him in the lift. He was drenched in sweat; his heart was beating furiously, his uniform glued to his skin.

'I'm Tim. Tim Mitchell,' a voice said, distant and echoing, as if from the far end of a tunnel.

With his half-opened eye Wingate saw a gathering shadow hovering over him. The voice and the shadow merged into a clean-shaven face which widened into a gleaming set of dry white teeth and a spongy, eager smile. 'I haven't had the honour of meeting you, Major Wingate. I just wanted you to know that I've heard of your campaign in Ethiopia. Indeed, I've read all your reports and I think . . .'

'Not now,' Wingate said. 'I need to get to my room.'

'Of course,' the colonel said. He pressed the button for the fifth floor. 'As a matter of fact I'm billeted right next door to you. I said as much this morning in a letter to Gwen. I hope you don't mind. I told her that I'd had the honour of living next door to Wingate of Ethiopia.'

Wingate didn't ask him who Gwen was, but Mitchell told him anyway. 'Gwen,' he announced, pulling out a photograph from his wallet, 'is my dear fiancé. We got engaged in Plymouth two weeks ago, just before I set sail for Egypt.'

'Colonel,' Wingate said weakly, 'what makes you think I care one jot about your private life?'

'That's rude, Wingate.'

But it also shut him up, which was all Wingate wanted. As the pneumatic lift made its slow ascent to the fifth floor, Wingate blacked out for a few seconds. But the young colonel didn't seem to notice this. Wingate's reputation, carved out of a series of outlandish myths and true but hard-to-credit exploits, had preceded him and, in Mitchell's eyes, his behaviour only served to confirm legends of the man's extreme eccentricity.

As they arrived at the fifth floor, Mitchell came out of his sulk. 'Major,' he said, 'how did you come up with the name Gideon Force?'

'Colonel,' Wingate said before leaping out, 'how did you come by such a perfectly dull mind?'

'Are you always this odious?'

'Only to toadying spies from GHQ.'

The world was starting to spin out of control. Wingate tried to get away from the colonel, to get to his room as quickly as possible. But he could barely see and could only barely stand upright, let alone walk. In the corridor, he careened into the wall, clung to it and began to slither towards the door to his room. Mitchell watched him first with irritation mixed with amusement then with concern.

'Is something the matter with you, Wingate?'

'Haven't you seen a man with malaria before?'

Mitchell grabbed hold of Wingate by the shoulders and swung him round. 'Your room is this way.' He guided him in the right direction. 'Have you seen a doctor?'

'Yes.' Wingate was trying to reach for his key.

Mitchell helped him insert the key into the lock. 'May I come into your room for a moment?'

'You may not. Why?'

'I was going to use your telephone to call a doctor.'

'I just told you that I've seen a doctor. I'll be fine once I'm rested.'

'Look here, Wingate. This is an order. I want you to leave your door unlocked.'

'Why?'

'So I can pop in once in a while and make sure you're all right.'

'Why is my welfare so important to you, Colonel?'

'You look pale as death. I want to make sure you're all

right. Then I'm going to have you arrested for rudeness to a superior officer.'

Wingate slammed the door shut. As he made to turn the key in the lock, the door pushed open and Mitchell's head appeared in the doorway.

'You're being quite paranoid, Wingate. I'm not a spy, and I'm not from GHQ.'

'Thank you, Colonel.'

'You're welcome, Major. Are you sure I shouldn't call a doctor?'

'I assure you, Colonel, I don't need to be seen by a doctor.'

'Very well. Remember I'm only next door. All you need do is tap on the wall and I'll be here in the blink of an eye.'

Wingate shut the door. He stood there and waited until he heard Mitchell's footsteps receding. He listened as Mitchell opened the door to the adjoining room.

Then, with painful step after painful step, he groped his way along the wall towards the bed at the far end of the room. He collapsed on the bed, rolled into the sheets and lay groaning with aches shooting through every limb in his body.

After tossing and turning for several minutes, Wingate crawled out of the sheets and reached out to the bedside table and picked up the lone file lying there. He flicked through the sheaves of loosely bound paper. It was a report he had written for General Headquarters on the conduct of the Ethiopian campaign; a furious, hastily written document tinged as much by memories of real and imagined slights as by the fever which was already laying siege on him when he sat down to write it.

Cynicism in this war will defeat us, but it is prevalent in our councils. Righteousness exalteth a nation.

He reached for a pen and began to cross out the second line. Then he thought better of it and decided to retain it.

He reached into his rucksack and pulled out a thermometer. Sucking on it, he went into the bathroom and stood in front of the shaving mirror.

You look pale as death, the irksome colonel had said. The man was right.

He removed the thermometer and read his temperature. That morning it had hovered between 100 and 103; then, before his foolish decision, born of restlessness, to go for a walk in the brutal noon-day heat had brought him to his present misery, the last two tablets of Atabrine had helped lower his temperature. Now it had risen to 104.

Atabrine, he thought, I must get some Atabrine.

He went back into the bedroom and picked up the telephone, dialled the hotel operator and asked to be put through to Tayib at the front desk.

'When's it coming?' Wingate asked when Tayib came on the line.

'Quite soon, Major.' He sounded evasive.

'How soon is quite soon, Tayib?'

'Within . . . within the hour, sir.'

Something in Tayib's voice made Wingate suspicious. He stared at the thermometer for a long while without saying another word.

'Are you there, Major Wingate?'

'Yes, Tayib, I'm here. I was just thinking . . .' He lapsed into further thought and then made up his mind. 'I was actually phoning to tell you that I no longer need the Atabrine. There's still some left of the dosage you got me yesterday. I'd simply misplaced the bottle. I've just found it; it was under the bed. Thank you, Tayib. Thank you for everything. Thanks to you, the Continental has lived up to its reputation of being a veritable oasis. Goodbye and God bless.'

'Are you leaving the hotel?' Tayib asked.

'No,' said Wingate. 'What makes you think that?'

'I just wondered, sir . . . you said goodbye.'

'I'm always saying goodbye, Tayib. I'm a soldier. It's an occupational reflex. I'm going to take a nap now. Please see to it that I'm not disturbed.'

'Of course, sir. Have a nice nap, sir.'

For a long while after he returned the phone to its cradle Wingate sat motionless on the bed. He picked up the thermometer and returned it to its pouch. Then he lifted the rucksack and carefully emptied its contents, including the thermometer he'd just placed into it, on the floor. He searched through the pile on the floor, searched every pocket sewn into the rucksack.

He was looking for his service pistol which he had in fact left behind in Addis Ababa in the haste and suddenness of his departure from Ethiopia.

He searched every corner of the room; under the bed, beneath the mattress, through drawers and wardrobe; he searched everywhere. But the pistol which he was convinced he'd seen and cleaned only a few days ago was nowhere to be found. He'd heard of a thriving black market in small arms and weapons in the City of the Dead – an ancient and sprawling graveyard, known also as the Cemetery of the Living, which housed not only dead Cairenes but hundreds of thousands of the destitute who lived in and amongst its monuments and burial chambers. He wondered if one of the cleaners had come upon the pistol and stolen it to boost the pittance of a take-home pay they received for the gruelling work they did and the long hours they were required to put in. But it didn't make sense that someone would steal a pistol and yet leave untouched all the cash he routinely left lying around the place.

He picked up the phone and began to dial the operator. Perhaps Tayib could help him come to the bottom of this little mystery of the missing pistol. The operator came on and Wingate began to ask to be put through to the front desk. Then he changed his mind.

As he put the phone down, Wingate's eyes fell on a hunting knife he'd picked up a year earlier in a market in Khartoum. He'd long given it up for lost, but it had lain all this time where he had thrown it on the day he bought it: in the rucksack whose contents now lay on the floor before him. He picked up the knife and went into the bathroom. He reached into his shaving bag and pulled out a tube of strop paste, squeezed a pinch into the palm of his hand and carefully worked it into the leather front of the strop hanging by the mirror. After he had thoroughly stropped the knife, he stood by the mirror, raising his chin so he could see the whole of his neck. He rubbed his fingers through his beard, as if he was about to shave it off.

Then, with all the strength he could summon, he plunged the knife into his neck. It sliced through flesh and tendon. As he proceeded to slaughter himself, with blood gushing out, he suddenly remembered the door. The door. He turned round, and with the knife firmly stuck to his windpipe, and parts of his brain beginning to die for lack of oxygen, Wingate went out of the bathroom. He reached the door and turned the key in the lock.

Satisfied, he headed back into the bathroom to finish what he had started. Standing in front of the mirror, he pulled out the knife, passed it to his other hand, and slashed at his jugular vein from another angle. Blood spurted out smearing the mirror. Wingate began to choke.

2

'When I hear a fellow lock a door, I don't think anything of it,' Colonel Mitchell said the next day in a letter to his fiancé. 'And if I hear him fall, that's his affair. But when I hear a fellow lock his door and then fall down . . .'

Immediately Mitchell heard the crash in the next room, he knew something was wrong. He was drifting off into a siesta when it happened. Still in his pyjamas, he ran out of his room into the corridor and knocked repeatedly on Wingate's door. There was no response. He called out Wingate's name; utter and complete silence. Thinking that he might have imagined it all, he tried opening the door. It certainly was locked. He made a dash for the lift. As always it took its time coming. He gave up waiting and bounded down the stairway.

When he arrived downstairs at the lobby and went to

the front desk to report the incident and to ask for a master key Mitchell was confronted by the sight of two army medics arriving there at the same time. They had come from the 15th Army Hospital on the other side of town to investigate a phone call they had received from the Continental Hotel half an hour earlier. Tayib, flustered and already regretting his decision to call them, was in the process of telephoning Wingate to warn him that he had visitors coming up to see him when Mitchell showed up in his pyjamas. It was Tayib's call to the army hospital and Mitchell's inability to mind his own business that came together to save Wingate's life.

When the medics, together with Mitchell, Tayib and the house manager, broke into Wingate's room, they found him unconscious on the floor, dying. There was blood everywhere.

The medics tried but failed to stop the bleeding. They rushed him in an ambulance across Cairo to the Army hospital. He was immediately operated upon, requiring a transfusion of nearly ten litres of blood.

Shortly after the operation was finished – the surgeons counted it a success – with the gashes in his throat neatly stitched, the malarial spasms returned. Unconscious and heavily anaesthetised, Wingate threw up everything in his stomach.

Ten tablets of Atabrine, whole, undigested, and almost as good as new, emerged with the soupy mess that came coughing out of his mouth.

The violent fit of vomiting re-opened the wounds and undid all the work the surgeons and nurses had done. They had to start all over. The anaesthesia began to wear off and towards the end of the second operation Wingate gradually regained consciousness and could feel the dull sting of every suture as it was threaded across his neck.

As he lay in hospital recovering from the deep wounds he had inflicted on himself, he spent his nights and days thinking of Ethiopia, and of Gideon Force, the small army with which he had put a decisive halt to Mussolini's dreams of empire.

3

One morning exactly five months and three days after Wingate failed to kill himself in Cairo, Japanese troops launched an amphibious assault on the British South East Asian colony of Malaya. On the same day, ninety minutes later, a fleet of bombers belonging to the Imperial Japanese Navy visited the Hawaiian island of Oahu and destroyed 188 planes belonging to the US Navy, killing thousands of American servicemen and civilians.

Twenty-four hours later, President Franklin Roosevelt signed a declaration of war against Japan. Two months later, Major Wingate was summoned out of the doghouse of a desk job into which he'd been cast after his fever-fuelled, Atabrine-induced suicide attempt and promoted a colonel.

General Wingate's task was to help kick the Japanese out of Burma.

He set about doing this by creating a cluster of long-range penetration groups trained to operate deep behind Japanese lines.

He named these rapid-reaction groups the Chindits.

I
HAILAKANDI

1

A swirling inferno appeared in the distance, a blue pillar of fire roaring towards them. Farabiti Banana, near the back of the slow-moving column marching in single file, froze briefly then shuffled along, nudged forward by the man behind him. The fire cut through the pitch-dark night and lit up the dense thicket of moss-covered trees and the rocks wrapped in lichen that rose into great hills and fell into steep valleys along their path filled with strange plants and nameless wild beasts, and snipers real and imagined whose imminent appearance had kept them moving since they left their last bivouac just before dawn, trailed by pi-dogs, and up till now, long after dusk, when their shoulders had sagged, crushed under the unbearable weight of the kit that each man carried on his back.

As the mast of flames whooshed towards them, Farabiti

Banana decided to run for his life. He felt it was neither his business nor his place to ask the man before him or the officer behind him why everyone but himself was behaving as if these flames, come to devour them, weren't there. He couldn't understand why they were all ignoring it, trudging on and ignoring it, consumed it seemed only by the sheer effort of will required to raise one foot in front of the other. Even the mules, who were not as wise as some men he'd come across, but a good deal wiser than others he had, did not appear concerned.

The impulse to flee vanished almost as soon as it crossed Farabiti Banana's mind. It dawned on him that the reason Samanja Damisa and Kyaftin Gillafsie and everyone else appeared so composed, the reason they all seemed so unmoved, was they knew they were trapped. They knew – even the mules knew – and he too should have known, that they had nowhere to run; the track along which they were marching lay between a shaggy hill which rose and sprawled several thousand metres and a green thicket behind which a precipice was concealed that would send man or mule who stepped over it plunging into a rock-strewn *chaung*, a fast-flowing stream, two thousand metres below.

Farabiti Banana remembered the words of the man they called the Janar.

'In quietness and confidence shall be your strength,' the Janar had said to them. 'The enemy will come at you with all he's got. He has one mission in Burma and one mission only. He's there to kill you. He's there to kill you for Emperor. He's there to kill you for General Tojo. He's there to kill you for Nippon. He's there to kill you or die trying. In his trenches every night and every morning, his commanders tell him that if his hands are broken, he should fight you with his feet. His commanders tell him that if his hands and feet are broken, he should fight you with his teeth. His commanders tell him that if he's taken prisoner when unconscious, he should stuff his tongue down his throat and choke himself to death. His commanders tell him that if there is no breath left in his body, he should fight you with his ghost. There's the measure of the enemy. Our mission in Burma is to insert ourselves inside his gut. Our victory is already half won, thanks to our training and our singleness of purpose. Now we must put our teaching into action and show that we can beat the Japanese wherever he may be. There will be no rest, no leave, no return until the battle has been won.

'Good luck and Godspeed,' said the Janar. 'In quietness and confidence shall be your strength.'

Farabiti Banana remembered those last words from the Janar's speech and wondered if those same words were running through the samanja's mind as he marched silently in front of him. Were all the others thinking the same thoughts? Did they think that walking quietly and confidently into these angry flames would earn them the Janar's esteem if they met him in the hereafter?

Farabiti Banana wiped his face with the back of his hand and realised he was trembling. His head felt heavy and his mouth tasted of bile. He was no stranger to fear but as he stood on that mountain track in the wildest reaches of the Burmese jungle that unhappy night five years into the Second World War, a long way away from the hamlet which he once called home, a village called Saminaka in Northern Nigeria where he was born less than seventeen years ago, Ali Banana knew he was about to die and a great terror took hold of his mind.

2

He stared at the back of Damisa's head and prayed the samanja would favour him with a look. Samanja Damisa was a tall, broad-chested man with an incongruously small head sprouting from a neck wide and solid like the trunk of a kuka tree. His face was marked by a ghastly scar which ran from his left ear to the ridge of his mouth. It made people look at him twice – the first time with shock, the second time with the shock intensified when they noticed he didn't have a left ear.

The missing ear lay somewhere in the east African city of Addis Ababa, withered and presumably turned to dust.

Three years earlier an Italian blackshirt, a member of the 400,000-strong expeditionary force sent to Abyssinia by Benito 'Il Duce' Mussolini, had found himself and twelve of his fellow *fascisti* caught in an ambush sprung upon them by a shadowy group called Gideon Force, an increasingly deadly guerrilla army of Africans led, the Italians knew, by a maverick British army colonel named Orde Charles Wingate, whose preferred mode of transport was the camel and who had been known to wear an alarm clock on his wrist, which would go off at appropriate moments throughout the day to remind him of things to do. In the ambush, the blackshirt found himself invested in hand-to-hand combat with Lance Kofur Abdulazeez Damisa, 23rd Nigeria Brigade, a fearsome giant with a scarified face. The Fascist soja proceeded to misalign the contours of Damisa's tribal-marks, and detach his ear, in a failed but spirited attempt to slice open the African's throat with an M38 Carcano bolt-action rifle fitted with a bayonet. The blackshirt went to his maker with his head detached from his body, and Lance Kofur Damisa searched in vain for his missing ear and was made a samanja. Later, when Gideon Force succeeded in kicking Il Duce's armies out of Abyssinia, Damisa was immortalised in a photograph shaking hands with Emperor Haile Selassie, his battle-battered face beaming with unabashed delight.

Samanja Damisa was Banana's hero. He was twelve years older than Banana and had been to more places and done more things than anyone Banana had met. He could say good morning and hello and what a lovely *panga* in Swahili, and many rude words in Italian, and you're so beautiful in Tigrinya and Amharic, and virtually anything he cared to say in English, barrack-French, market-Yoruba or town-Fulani. His mother tongue, which was also Ali Banana's, was Hausa.

And it was in Hausa that he would frequently and with great patience explain things to Farabiti Banana, whose English was only 'small-small' but who dived to the ground faster than anyone else present the first time he heard the cry 'Take cover!' This happened during one of their training sessions in India on a base near the north-eastern district of Hailakandi, a day after Banana was sent from GHQ West Africa in Chiringa to join 12th Battalion, Nigeria Regiment.

3

Before Banana joined 12th NR, he had been in a Bombay military hospital for a week, left there by his own battalion, the 5th NR, to recover from an ill-timed bout of chicken-pox. By the time he was rid of the harmless but unsightly pores and certified fit to rejoin his battalion, they were already in Burma, and had fired the first of many shots in anger. This involved routing a Japanese company at a cost of one platoon. They also survived an ambush, losing five mules, with two men severely wounded, and an elephant that charged into the jungle with its mahout on top.

Banana left Bombay and travelled by train to Chiringa, a town in the Bengal region, where the West African Base and Rear Headquarters resided. In Chiringa he was told that 5th NR would send for him when time, the complex logistics of troop deployment and the thorny issue of space on C-47 Dakotas coincided to avail them of the means of delivering him to them. In other words, they were doing fine without him, thanks for asking.

Banana waited at the base for a whole month and heard not a word. He paid a visit to Staff Office every day without fail, begging, pestering and haranguing the non-commissioned officers there.

He haughtily informed the NCOs that he hadn't travelled all the way from Kaduna to Laagos, from Laagos to Preetown, from Preetown to Darban and all the way to India just so he could go back to Nigeria with tales of chickenpox conquered.

'I here for to fight na Boma,' Banana declared. 'I here for to killi di Janpani.'

Instead he found himself eating curry morning, day and night. He had never seen so much food in his life. One morning he turned up at Staff Office, marched straight to the Hausa NCO on duty, gave him a salute that was brisk but faultless in its execution and then proceeded to blame him for everything that had gone wrong for him since he arrived in India. The three NCOs watching this exchange asked their Nigerian counterpart what Farabiti Banana, whose eloquent and impassioned diatribe was delivered in Hausa, was saying, and why was the sepoy slapping himself repeatedly in the stomach?

The Nigerian NCO, a mild-mannered man who had been a primary school teacher in Jos, explained the situation to them.

'Rifleman Banana,' he told them, 'holds me responsible for turning him into a glutton.'

'Is Banana really his name?' asked the Gold Coaster.

'I'm afraid it is. His name is Ayaba, which in Hausa means banana. Private Banana says it's my fault he's grown a paunch. Every time he comes here to ask about re-joining his battalion, he says, I fob him off by sending him to the canteen. He wants to go to Burma. He will go on hunger strike unless we arrange for him to join his battalion in Burma.'

This was obviously serious.

'Why can't he join them?' asked the Gambian NCO.

'No reason whatsoever,' the Nigerian said with a sigh. 'But his platoon won't have him back. They're convinced he'll give them chickenpox. I've tried explaining to them that he's now completely free of it and couldn't possibly infect anyone. I've sent them his Medical Board report but they're having none of it. Ignorance. Ignorance and superstition. But you know our people.'

'Have you explained this to Sepoy Banana?'

'I've explained to him –' The Nigerian NCO coughed and cleared his throat. 'I've explained to Sepoy Banana that his platoon . . . is heartily waiting to see him.'

'In other words, you lied in your throat,' said the Sierra Leonean.

'The boys in his group are all from the same village,' explained the Nigerian samanja. 'They think he's a wonder-ful chap but they're terrified of catching chickenpox. Their OC is of the opinion that the morale of his men comes before all else. To that end, he's personally promised to make sure I lose my stripes if my chubby friend here were somehow to magic his way back to 5th NR. What the lieutenant didn't tell me was what on earth to do with the pregnant little bugger.'

'And Sepoy Banana is determined to see action?'

'Completely hell-bent.'

'There's a true infantryman for you,' said the Sierra Leonean, looking fondly at Farabiti Banana. 'You know that saying: "The only way you get out of the Infantry is on a stretcher or six feet under." Here's a chap who takes it to heart.'

The Gambian ran his hand through his prematurely thinning hair.

'I think I've got just the solution,' he said. 'Let's send him to Hailakandi.'

'Hailakandi?' said the Sierra Leonean. It wasn't really a question. 'You mean, send him to the Chindits?'

'Why not?' said the Gambian.

'But the Chindits, Sergeant. The Chindits.'

'What about them, Havildar?' A havildar was the Indian Army equivalent of a sergeant.

'Havildar, can you see this fine specimen of a soldier, with a stomach the size of a conga, marching a thousand miles across Burma? That's how far every man on the last Chindit expedition had to cover on foot. And each of them carrying kit weighing eighty pounds.'

'I don't know,' said the Gambian. 'What I do know is that 12th NR in Hailakandi is one man short of a crisis in their Animal Transport platoon. What does your man know about mules?'

The Nigerian NCO asked Farabiti Banana what he knew about mules.

'The sepoy knows nothing about mules. Although –' he paused to listen to Farabiti Banana, whose eyes had lit up at the question, 'he once had dreams of owning a horse. He saved up for it for many years but was then presented with a donkey by a scoundrel who took his money under false pretences. He brought the matter before the village chief but he should have known it was a waste of time. The chief and the scoundrel were related by marriage.'

'What was that about the chief's clerk?' asked the Gambian who had picked up a few words of Hausa from Nigerian traders in Banjul. 'He said *dan kilaki*.'

'*Dan kilaki* means son-of-a-clerk,' explained the Nigerian. 'It's a Hausa term of abuse. It means son-of-a-woman-who-trades-her-body-for-money.'

'Nigerian clerks are prostitutes?' wondered the Sierra Leonean.

'It's a term of abuse,' the Nigerian archly replied.

'What did the sepoy do with his donkey?' asked the Gambian, anxious to avoid a quarrel.

'He fitted it with saddle and bridle and rode it like a horse,' said the Nigerian. 'It served him well and in time he came to realise that God had used the scoundrel to gift him with a loyal servant. Unfortunately, the donkey was stolen by a marauding band of –'

'*Kafirai tsirara a kan kafirin dokuna*,' declared Farabiti Banana, swiping a fly off his nose.

'Stark naked infidels on exceptionally fast horses,' the

Nigerian NCO translated, word for word. 'They were from a neighbouring village. You may well ask, he says, what in God's name a bunch of infidels naked as their wild horses would want with a mere donkey. Well, he says, they ate the donkey, that's what they did with it. They made a tasty feast of it, the Godless cads.'

After that, Banana sank into a dejected silence. But not for long.

'Why is Samanja Mackaley asking Farabiti Banana about mules?' he demanded. He had a slightly disconcerting way of suddenly speaking of himself in the third person.

'I keep reminding you, private, I'm a sergeant, not a sergeant major,' said Samanja Mackaley.

'By the grace of the Holy Prophet Muhammad – may blessing and Divine regard be upon him – every samanja is a samanja,' Banana imperiously informed him in a tone that indicated that he had no further interest in arguing the matter.

Samanja Mackaley shook his head in great wonderment and turned to the other three-chevron samanjas.

'12th NR lost a muleskinner to a cobra last week,' he said. 'I suggest we send Private Banana as a replacement.'

'Mules?' Ali gasped as if he'd been stung by a driver ant. 'Do you know who I am? I'm the son of Dawa the king of well-diggers whose blessed nose could sniff out water in Sokoto while he's standing in Saminaka. I'm the son of Hauwa whose mother was Talatu whose mother was Fatimatu queen of the moist kulikuli cake, the memory of whose kulikuli still makes old men water at the mouth till this day. Our people say that distance is an illness; only

37

travel can cure it. Do you think that Ali Banana, son of Dawa, great-grandson of Fatima, has crossed the great sea and travelled this far, rifle strapped to his shoulder, to look after mules?'

4

Three days later, Farabiti Banana, travelling by rickshaw, train and by truck, and sulking all the way, arrived in Hailakandi. He went straight to the first officer he saw and launched into a speech.

'Kyaftin, sir,' Banana began. 'Let me ask you this question: does anything in my carriage mark me out as a drover? Does Ali Banana look to you like a mule-driver? I ask you these questions, Kyaftin, sir, because your men in Chiringa have told me that my skills as a marksman, for which I was invited to this land by your great master Kingi Joji himself, are no longer needed. I'm now to spend my days looking after a mule. Ask anyone, Kyaftin, sir, I'm not mean. I'm not one to say, "Roast me a cassava and you can have the skin." But, Kyaftin, sir, if you take away my gun and put me in charge of your mule, as God is

God and the Prophet His prophet, that mule will suffer. It will suffer, Kyaftin. It will suffer so much that on the day of judgement, when it hears that I, Ali Banana, have been admitted to heaven, "Not if I'd been there," is what the mule will say. I haven't said anything now that I haven't said before. Your men in Chiringa merely laughed at me and hurried me along to this place. But their laughter did not bother me. When they laughed at me I was like the pot in the tale of the scorpion and the pot: "It's such an unfeeling world," said the scorpion when he tried to sting the pot. On the other hand, I pay homage to the scorpion for, as the saying goes, he who spurns that which is short hasn't stepped on a scorpion. Am I being spurned because I'm short? It surely cannot be because I don't speak your language. I've tried learning it, your eminence, God is my witness. But every time I start from a to z I get lost somewhere between β and δ, and my head hurts and I have to lie down to recover. May you live long, Kyaftin, sir.'

The kyaftin's sleepless eyes dwelled on Farabiti Banana for a long time after he'd finished speaking. The kyaftin looked either irritated or amused. Banana couldn't tell. The kyaftin swung round on his heels and called out to a tall, bulky man with a missing ear who was busy cleaning a rifle outside one of the many bashas dotted across the base, swinging in the wind like so many ears of wheat. The one-eared samanja carefully laid down the gun and wiped the sweat off his face with an orange handkerchief. He strode toward them, passing through the crowds of British, Burmese, Nepalese and Nigerian officers and men rushing to and fro, and the mules and ponies purposefully wandering about the base, all caught in a dusty, sweat-drenched atmosphere of recoiled tension.

'Sergeant, did we ask for a muleteer from Chiringa?' the kyaftin asked the samanja in impeccable Hausa.

The samanja stood tall and rigid, towering over both the kyaftin and Farabiti Banana whose shock at the kyaftin's Hausa had rendered him speechless.

'Not that I know of, sir,' said the samanja.

'Private Banana,' said the kyaftin. 'Is that a Zazzau accent I detect? Are you from Zaria?'

Banana leapt into the air with delight and his tongue, no longer tied, spilled out with words.

'How did the kyaftin know?' he gushed. 'I was born in Saminaka. But when I was seven years old my father sent me to Zaria to learn the blacksmith's trade. My master was a hard man.'

He unbuttoned his khaki shirt and displayed the saw-like welts engraved on his back by his master's horsewhip.

'But I called no other place home until six months ago when my two best friends, Yusufu and Iddrisi, whose master Suleiman the tinker was an even greater pestilence than mine, came to me one night as I sat under the kuka tree behind the compound of Abu-the-butcher's son Hamza, who is himself a butcher also, as was his grandfather and his father before him. I was sitting under that tree right behind Hamza's compound, enjoying the breeze and thanking God for creating stars of such beauty to ease the misery of my existence, for just before the call to prayer that very evening, my back had tasted of my master's

41

strap. "Ali," said Yusufu and Iddrisi, "have you heard the story of the day?" Well, it so happened I'd just left the village square where Gizo-gizo, the albino hunchback, had been spinning another of his delightful twilight tales. Thinking that their master had caused them to miss Gizo-gizo as punishment for some trifle or the other, for that man's pettiness was only rivalled by master's, I did to them as they would have done to me if I had missed the albino's tale: I crossed my feet, broke a kola nut and shared it round, praising the name of God, the Merciful and the Beneficent, and proceeded to tell them that night's tale as I remembered it.

'To begin the story I said, "In the name of God the Compassionate, the Merciful," and "May the peace of God be upon him, after whom there is no prophet. One day," I said, "a woman was walking with her son when a bird flying overhead dropped its droppings on her head. Mother and child went on their way until they came to a herd of cattle and there the boy saw the dung lying thick on the grass. 'Mother,' said the boy, 'isn't it a good thing that God didn't put cows up in the sky?' "That is all," I said. "Off with the rat's head."

'But when I finished telling them the story, instead of thanks or even a smile all I got for my effort was a whack on the head. "Fool," they said, "that's not the story of the day." Well, I had to admit, the hunchback's telling of the tale was much better. But who in the world can tell a tale as well as Gizo-gizo the honey-voiced albino hunchback? "Fool," they said, "forget about Gizo-gizo. The story of the day is that Kingi Joji, monarch of Ingila, is fighting

42

a war in a land called Boma and he wants our help. He wants all able-bodied men to go to Kaduna and join his band of warriors." Well, if truth be told, I was quite surprised at Kingi Joji's request and up till that night I'd never heard of this land called Boma. Neither had Yusufu and Iddrisi, but they had already made up their minds to answer the king's summon and go to Kaduna. All they wanted to know before setting out was if I wanted to go with them. My tale is long but I'll make it short. That very night, Yusufu, Iddrisi and I set out on foot and headed, as the crow flies, in the direction of Kaduna.'

But he hadn't quite finished. He went on to tell them everything that had happened to him since he'd arrived in India six weeks earlier with Yusufu, Iddrisi and all the other young men from Zaria who had rushed to answer Kingi Joji's call once they saw Ali and his two friends, home to show off a few weeks after joining the army, in their smart khaki drills: the sandy-green shirt with black, palm-tree buttons, the 'long-shorts' that stopped just beyond the knees, and the furry green fez with a tassel on top. And for their feet, the men were issued with a specially – some officers mumbled, hastily – designed 'tropical style' boot which was broad and rounded at the sides, and suggested the shape of a boat. Indeed when Ali and his friends marched, proudly, through the streets of Kaduna in these boots, they looked as if they were wearing a flotilla of shoe-sized boats and could set sail if they stepped into the River Kaduna and the wind was strong enough.

Ali, whose tiny feet had known no shoes before, wore them with great pride. His ritual every morning consisted of dawn prayer, drill, breakfast and shoeshine. He would pick up the boots one foot at a time, wipe off the soft coat of dust with a damp rag; dab a drop or two of groundnut oil on a ball of cotton wool and buff the shoe till it shone like the mirror in the officers' mess. He was so proud of his shoes, and so eager to show them off, he soon devised a better way to present them to his public: instead of wearing them on his feet – or rather, truth be told, because he found bare-footing much more comfortable – he took to hanging the boots by their laces around his neck. This proved so popular with the public that soon, and to the mild sorrow of the British officers, it became the fashion among the men to wear their shoes not on their feet but around their necks. In certain parts of Kaduna that year, a town where everyone knew someone who had been specially invited to Boma by Kingi Joji to teach the Janpani what's what, no self-respecting young man of means would step on his Raleigh bicycle on a night out without his barrack-necklace, as it became known, shining from his neck.

5

'Where did he learn to speak Hausa so well?' Banana asked Damisa later that night as he prepared his bamboo mat in the corner of the basha that the samanja had assigned to him.

'Who?'

'Kyaftin Gillafsie.'

'In Hausaland.'

He noticed a mat in another corner of the tent. 'Whose mat is that?'

'Pash.'

'He's not here.'

'Well observed.'

'Where is he?'

'Sentry duty.'

'He must have been there for quite a while.'

'What are you talking about?' The samanja was trying to sleep.

'Kyaftin Gillafsie. To have learnt Hausa so well.'

'Long enough.'

'He doesn't speak like a white man.'

'Doesn't he?'

'No. He speaks just like us.'

'That may be because he was born in Kano.'

'Ah! Well, that explains it, doesn't it?'

'That's why he didn't toss you right back to Chiringa where I have no doubt they could have found better use for you than we possibly could here. If Kyaftin Gillafsie has one major fault, it's that he's got too much of a good heart.'

'How can that be a fault, Samanja?'

'Well, for one thing, he doesn't have to put up with your non-stop blather while he's trying to catch some sleep before stand-to.'

'What is stand-to?'

'You've brought yourself all the way from Zaria to fight for Kingi Joji and you don't know what stand-to means?'

'The things I don't know, Samanja – God arm you with a prosperous hand – will fill a book twice as big as the Holy Book – May God, who put those words on my lips and who will surely hold me to account for them, forgive me. Have I offended you, Samanja?'

'What makes you think you have?'

'Then why do you keep talking to me as if I were a child? You've all but ignored me since we met this afternoon. You haven't once looked me in the eye.'

'How old are you?'

'Old enough to be in the army, Samanja, sir. God give you four wives – if you don't already have four. And forty children – assuming you don't already have forty. And the wealth to keep them all in splendour.'

'You're quite a character, aren't you? How old are you, Farabiti?'

'Seventeen last Ramadan.'

'How old are you, Farabiti?'

Farabiti Banana's voice broke. 'Sixteen, Samanja. I'm sixteen years of age.'

Samanja Damisa had been talking with his back turned to Banana.

'You do look sixteen,' he said. Then he continued, 'But really, Farabiti, how old are you?'

Finally admitting defeat, his voice dropping to a whisper, Banana said, 'I was born on the eighth day of the month of Ramadan in the year 1348, which was a Jumma'a.'

Damisa made a quick mental sum. Friday the 7th of February, 1930.

Now Damisa turned on his mat and looked at Banana across the tent.

'That makes you thirteen, Farabiti.'

'Fourteen . . . in a few months time,' pleaded Banana.

He was hunched over on his mat, his head resting on his bent knees, his hands clutching at his legs. 'You won't tell the kyaftin, will you? Please don't tell him. Please don't tell anyone. That will be the end of me if you tell. They'll send me back home.' He was shaking. 'They'll send me home,' he repeated unhappily.

47

'Stop crying, Ali,' Damisa said gently. 'Wanting to be a man is no sin.'

'But that wasn't why I joined up,' Banana said disconsolately. 'I joined up because of Yusufu and Iddrisi. We grew up together. They, like me, had been sent to Zaria when they were but children and even though they were a few years older than me, they were my best friends. I don't know any of my brothers or sisters. Yusufu and Iddrisi are the only brothers I know. I joined up only because they did. '

'That,' said Damisa 'is as good a reason as any.'

But kindness seemed only to throw Banana into greater despair. He wept heartily now, throwing his arms about in the air and wailing.

'There was something I didn't tell the kyaftin today,' he said when he'd stopped crying. 'I didn't tell him that I knew why Yusufu and Iddrisi and the others didn't send for me from Burma when I was in Chiringa. The NCOs kept telling me that it was because there was no room on any of the supply planes leaving from the base every day and going to the front. What they didn't know was that when I was in hospital with that terrible chickenpox in Bombay, Yusufu and Iddrisi visited me just before they left for Burma. They'd been telling me since before we left Nigeria and all through the journey to India that they didn't feel it was right that I'd joined the army. It wasn't the fact that I'd lied about my age to get in that bothered them. It was because they thought I was still a child. They said it was wrong that a boy my age should be going to fight in Burma.'

'Didn't they know how old you were the night they asked you to come with them to join the army?'

'Well,' said Ali sheepishly. 'They didn't really ask me to come with them that night. In fact, they laughed in my face when I asked if I could come with them. I had to wait a whole month before I made my own way to Kaduna and went to the recruitment station. They were not pleased when they found out I had joined up. They even threatened to tell the OC that I'd lied about my age, but I knew they wouldn't. And even if they did, it was their word against mine. After all, on the day I joined, there were pagans in the queue with me, who merely shrugged when the scribe-samanja asked them their age and said they didn't know; and the scribe-samanja would measure them with his eyes and say, "I'll write down eighteen." Or "My idiot nephew is eighteen. You share the same height and you're bulkier than the lazy son-of-a-clerk so I'll write down nineteen." I hadn't even gone there with the intention of lying. It was only when I heard the scribe-samanja shouting angrily at the man in front of me that my heart sank into the ground underneath my feet. "So what if you have a beard?" The scribe-samanja shouted at the man in front of me. "My he-goat has a beard. Does that make him sixteen? Stupid son-of-a-clerk, come back next year." And so learning from this fellow's misfortune – he didn't look a day older than twelve, the poor wretch – I told the scribe-samanja that I was seventeen. He said I looked sixteen. I said his goat must be older than me since I didn't have a whisker to speak of, let alone a beard. He laughed, calling me a son-of-a-clerk, but I let it pass; my mother's honour is sacred to me but I knew she would understand, and I hadn't walked from Zaria all the way to Kaduna to trade insults with a man who had a rifle lying by his feet. After he finished laughing at me, he asked for my name, the village I was from, and whether I'd ever suffered from the ailment of the cold and if I was cured, and how many wives I had. I gave him my name and told him where I was from. As to his last three questions, I also told him the truth: that I had no spouse and that I'd found no reason to seek release from an ailment which had never caught me in its snare. I stood there watching him commit everything I said to his ledger. At last he said, "The tailor-samanja's junior mistress had twins this morning so you'll have to wait until he returns tomorrow to fit you for your livery. But the boots-samanja is over there. Go and get your feet sized up." But, Samanja, from the day I joined up, Yusufu and Iddrisi had their mind set against me. And I didn't help matters much when I asked them what they'd told the scribe-samanja when he asked them about the illness of the cold. For that chill, yellow discharge from the penis had sent them both scurrying in agony to the house of Hajia Binta-the-herbalist not once but twice that year alone. Needless to say, the affliction had come their way from the house of Jummai-the-clerk who married a different man every night and sometimes two men if the first one had tried the old trick on her of saying he'd forgotten his wallet at the barber's. But I only brought up the matter of the prostitute and the clap they got from her to show Yusufu and Iddrisi that I too could keep a secret. It shut them up until we got on the big boat and travelled to India. We had scarcely set foot on land when my whole body was covered in pores. Then they said to me, "See? God had a whole shipload to choose from, but who alone among us does He punish with chickenpox?" That was the last time I spoke to them.'

'But you said they came to see you at the hospital.'

'That was just before 5th NR were flown out to Burma. They did come to see me but I left them to do all the talking. What they'd come to tell me was that they and all the other boys from Zaria had put their heads together and decided that when I left hospital I must own up to the officers at Bombay HQ and tell them that I'd lied about my age. For my own benefit, they said, they would tell our company OC, and everyone who cared to listen, that they were afraid I would give them chickenpox if I came back. They would tell all the white officers that they believed I would jinx the section, on top of infecting them, if I was allowed back.'

'Why didn't you own up when you left hospital?'

'I almost did. But then I decided that if I was good enough to be the best marksman in the platoon when we were in training in Kaduna then I was old enough to carry a gun and fight the Janpani. And I really was the top marksman in the platoon, God is my witness.'

'Oh well,' he sighed sadly, seemingly resigned to his fate. 'I suppose it's a court martial for me now.'

Samanja Damisa looked at Banana in the dim light of the hurricane lantern in the middle of the tent. 'A boy is a man when he feels he's a man. A man at forty can remain a child if he hasn't decided to be a man. I was barely fourteen when I got my first job. Your secret is safe with me.'

'May God crown your head with success,' Banana said, his eyes welling again.

Banana was effusive with gratitude and it took him no time to find his boisterous self again. 'The NCOs in Chiringa,' he declared, 'said that this regiment was part of a special battalion called Eat-Something-or-the-other.' The Hausa word for eat is ci, pronounced with an 'h' between the two letters.

'Chindits,' said Damisa, already beginning to regret the promise he'd just made.

'That's it. I knew it had something to do with eating.'

'It has nothing to do with eating.'

As if on cue, Banana's stomach gave a loud rumble.

'There is some kulikuli in that bag over there by the wall.' Damisa said, shaking his head. 'Help yourself to it.'

Banana could not believe his ears. 'Kulikuli here in India? God is truly great.'

As he crunched the delicious groundnut balls between his teeth, he kept shaking his head in wonder and breaking into delighted peals of laughter.

'Did you bring them all the way from home?' he asked.

'Farabiti Danja brought it with him. It was his mother's parting gift.'

'You'd be surprised what some of the boys tried to bring along on the journey,' Banana said, chewing loudly and burping as he chewed. 'While we were at sea over a hundred pounds of dawadawa were found under Aminu Yerwa's bed after the men sharing his cabin started complaining of a foul smell. The dawadawa had gone bad in the airless cabin and there were maggots gathering inside it.' Dawadawa, a seasoning made from fermented locust beans, was pungent enough even when fresh. 'When the OC asked Aminu why he'd brought so much with him he said he'd been hoping to keep some for himself and to sell the rest in small portions to the boys when we got to India.'

Damisa groaned. He'd heard a dozen variations on that story. But that wasn't why he groaned. Instead of sating his hunger and sending him to sleep, the kulikuli had sharpened Banana's tongue and now it seemed he could go on for ever.

'I heard so many Hausa voices when I was looking for the mess tonight —' Banana announced, shifting sideways to release a loud fart which he attributed, with evident satisfaction, to the wonderful kulikuli. 'I thought I was back in Kaduna again.' It was clear that he was about to launch into another story.

'Farabiti?' Damisa said.

'Yes, Samanja?'

'Does your mouth ever stop talking?'

'Only when I'm asleep. But even then —'

'Go to sleep, Farabiti. Go to sleep.' Damisa leaned forward and blew out the lantern.

'But I talk even in my sleep. I say all sorts of things,' Banana said in the darkness. Then he added, 'Thank you, Samanja, for being so kind to me. I've got just two questions then I'll leave you alone.'

'What are they?'

'The first question is this. The Chiringa samanjas said

53

the Chindits were going on a special operation. What is this special operation?'

'No one knows. What is in no doubt is that we are going to Burma. When we go and where in Burma, no one knows. What's your second question?'

'The job you got when you were fourteen.'

'What about it?'

'What was it?'

'It was nothing really, merely prison work.'

'You were a prison warder when you were fourteen?'

'Not exactly a warder.'

'What were you?'

'I worked in the row of death. I was an apprentice executioner at Sokoto Prison.'

Banana laughed nervously. 'You're just trying to scare me.'

'No, I'm not,' said Damisa. 'Sleep well, Farabiti.'

Not another word came out of Banana's lips for the rest of that night. Not even when he was asleep.

6

The next seven days went in something of a blur – the exercises were gruelling and all-consuming; by the end of each day Banana passed out as soon as he returned to the tent and staggered to his mat. Stand-to seemed to come increasingly earlier each day and the exercises seemed to go on for much longer. By the end of that week there had not been a night when he got more than three hours of sleep. Banana's stomach rebelled several times.

By the end of the second week, Banana had stopped throwing up.

Then a persistent looseness of the bowels, combined with spells of dizziness, threatened to undo him. One morning he caught sight of himself in a mirror and found that his face, jet-black since the day he was born, was turning yellow. He ran straight for the medics' tent, changed course half-way there as his stomach suddenly announced its intention to soil his trousers, and ended up frantically pacing about at the back of a very long queue of incontinent men with yellowing faces also desperately awaiting their turn to use the pit latrines. As he writhed in the queue, buttocks firmly pressed together, he watched those emerging from the latrines and noticed that they too had a yellow discoloration of the skin.

Godiwillin Nnamdi, a school-teacher's son from Onitsha who had joined the army to spite his father for some slight he could no longer remember, ominously announced that only last week two Indian nationalists, who wanted neither the British in their country, nor the Japs, but would prefer the Japs if they had to make a choice, had been caught trying to poison the base's water supply. Godiwillin wrote about it in a letter to his parents. His father wrote back saying he only wished Godiwillin had followed his advice and used his first school-leaving certificate to become a teacher instead of a killer of men. He told him that his sister Blessing had just received her nursing certificate and his brother Godwin had entered St Paul's Seminary in Igbariam, and that the whole family remembered him every night at bedtime prayer. The reply never got past the censor and Godiwillin never saw it.

Bloken Yahimba, a Tiv from Gboko, said he'd also heard the story but it was a latrinograph; a story started, as stories often were, while the men were squatted side by side answering nature. Bloken's full name was Jerome 'Broken Bottles' Yahimba. Jerome, eighteen on his next birthday, had been bald since the day he was born. He acquired the nickname 'Broken Bottles' in his wild teenage years – precisely between the ages of fourteen and sixteen – when he used to smash shards of broken bottles on his bald head just to see the look on people's faces. Bloken's tongue sometimes had the habit of replacing the letter *r* with the letter *l*. As a result of this peculiarity of speech, he rejoiced in the name Jelome 'Bloken Bottles' Yahimba. He was known as Jelome for a while but he preferred to be called Bloken, and that was the name under which he joined the army.

Haliyu Danja, a wag from the fishing village of Argungu, instantly transformed the diarrhoea-propelled wriggling movement of his feet into an ecstatic dance which he named the tape-worm spasm. Danja, whose name was pronounced Danger because that really was the correct spelling of the invented name he'd claimed as his own to the earnest and over-worked men at the recruitment station in his home village, professed to know the cause of their yellowing faces and upset stomachs. The cause, he announced sagely, was the four tablets they were all required to take daily. Danja omitted to add that this was the medics' advice, he'd just been to see them. The medics had told him that he and half the men and officers on the base were suffering from the side-effects of Mepacrine, the new anti-malarial drug they had been instructed to issue the sojas.

By the end of the third week, Banana's body had learnt to love Mepacrine; the dizziness went, he no longer had the runs, and only occasionally did a sallow face stare back at him when he chanced upon a mirror. His pot belly disappeared.

He learnt not so simple things such as covering tracks, the art of evasion, watermanship, river crossing, the open-eyed science of appreciating your terrain, night operations, defensive operations, stealth operations, initiating action on contact with the enemy; squad, platoon and column tactics, navigating the jungle, patrolling, scouting and map-reading, and preparing landing zones for airdrops. Together with every member of his unit, including the muleteers, he learnt to use every weapon in his section.

Many of the sessions were taught by specialists. But a great deal of the instruction came from officers and NCOs who themselves had spent several months at a Bush Warfare school where they gained the skills and were trained to teach them.

He learnt things he thought he already knew, such as the proper way to clean a rifle.

'Before you start cleaning your rifle,' said Samanja Damisa, grabbing hold of Haliyu Danja's Lee-Enfield to demonstrate, 'always make sure the cartridge is empty. When you've checked it's unloaded, then inspect the bore. Open the action and check for spots stained by powder or lead. In a bolt-action rifle like this chap here, remove the bolt. Inspect the bore by holding the muzzle towards a light. Look from chamber to muzzle; if there's any trace of rust or lead use a swab to wipe the bore. Then run a patch – make sure it's dry – through the bore. Run another patch through it just to make sure, then use a slightly oiled patch to finish the job. Clean the inside of the receiver, also the face of the breechblock. Now disassemble the rifle and clean all the parts using patches and brushes.

And finally,' said the samanja, 'apply a light coat of oil to protect it. Then, with great care, reassemble it. And, boys, your rifle should be as good as new. Repeat the process every single day. Make it a habit, the first thing you do when you wake up. Clean your rifle at the first opportunity every time after you've used it, and particularly when you haven't used it for some time.'

The men listened politely, careful to hide their boredom. There was nothing Damisa had said or done that they didn't already know about cleaning a rifle. Even Banana felt his time would have been better spent practising Haliyu Danja's spasm dance.

'I know what you're all thinking.' Damisa said with a knowing smile. 'You think I'm wasting your time, don't you? Well, let's see now,' he fixed his gaze on the man swaying gently beside Banana, 'Farabiti Zololo will now use his No. 4 Mark 1 to show us how to clean a rifle.'

Zololo stirred from his slumber, stepped forward, unslung his rifle and proceeded to clean it. It appeared to Banana that he did it flawlessly. He himself would have done it the same way. It was exactly as Damisa had shown them. But the samanja wasn't impressed. 'Do it again, Dogo,' he said to Zololo, calling him by his nickname. Again Zololo took the rifle apart, cleaned it, oiled it, and put it back together. Damisa still wasn't satisfied.

'What is Farabiti Zololo doing wrong?' he asked the men.

They all looked blankly at him. He turned to Zololo. 'Why didn't you check to see if it was loaded before you started cleaning it?'

'I knew it was unloaded,' Zololo said bristling. 'I unloaded it myself this morning.' Zololo had been a kofur but had been stripped of his stripes after a fight in Katsina with a Malian trader over a gambling debt.

'I asked Farabiti Zololo first because I know him to be a fine soja,' Damisa said to them. 'We fought side-by-side during the East African Campaign, so I should know. But even good sojas make mistakes. When you pick up a firearm,' he said, lifting Danja's rifle for them all to see, 'always assume that it is loaded. Even if you know it isn't. Always handle it with the same level of care that you would if it was loaded. If you don't, boys, one day you'll pick up your rifle to clean it, knowing that it is empty. And you'll press the trigger by accident and that one bullet that you somehow missed when you emptied the cartridge that morning will burst out and make a hole the size of a fist on your head. It will be the last time you clean a rifle.'

7

At the beginning of the following month, shortly after Banana turned fourteen, they had a visit from the man everyone called the Janar. The visit happened as the men were having supper in the open air one night, under a full moon. Banana was sitting across from Samanja Damisa and Farabiti Zololo listening to them reminisce about a splendid battle that happened in a place called Babile Gap in Abyssinia back in '41.

Zololo was in mid-speech recounting the highlight of this episode of the East African Campaign when he suddenly stopped talking, his eyes glued to a spot behind Banana.

'The Janar,' he said, 'he is here.' His voice was filled with wonder. Everyone pushed their plates aside. An awed silence descended on the officers and men.

Banana turned round and saw a man no taller than himself, perhaps slightly shorter even. The man ambled rather awkwardly into the middle of the gathering, his hands clasped behind his back. His tunic was creased and untidy; it looked as if he slept in it, washed in it and hadn't stepped out of it since the day he stepped into it a considerably long time ago. He wore a beard that was full and black and wildly unkempt. Underneath the olive-green African sun-helmet perched incongruously on his head that moonlit night, his eyes, a blistering blue, were set deep in their sockets, moving frantically and then narrowing into sharp, unblinking focus; and when they settled on a man it was as if they could see through his flesh and into his mind. But he looked tired and his shoulders, which were quite broad, stooped slightly so that as he walked unhurriedly across the dusty clearing where the men were gathered, he looked as though he might suddenly keel over and fall asleep.

When the Janar spoke, his voice was raspy and he had a vague stutter. Occasionally, his hands would rise and scratch a messy scar on his neck that looked as if it had been taken apart and restitched, hurriedly, by someone with hands that shook badly as they held the scalpel. But the words rushed out of the Janar's mouth in whole, fully formed sentences and he seemed to speak without pausing for breath. When he spoke, and as he continued speaking, he was transformed from the awkward, slightly hesitant man of moments ago, into a man possessed. And when he finished half an hour later – though it felt more like ten minutes – and shuffled into the night, seemingly all too fragile again, they too were possessed by his visions and drunk on his words.

8

D-Section, Damisa's own little section, stayed up that night talking about the Janar's visit. They all abandoned their quarters and headed for Damisa's basha. Only six of them were present, – Godiwillin was on sentry duty and Bloken was in sickbay, down with tonsillitis. The meeting did not start well.

What almost soured the evening was a row that started between Zololo and Pash and almost came to blows, spreading so that soon angry words were flying from every corner of the tent.

Of those present in Damisa's basha that night, only Zololo and Damisa had set eyes on the Janar before. Zololo had seen him only from afar during Emperor Haile Selassie's victory parade into Addis Ababa after the occupying Italian army had been kicked out. The Janar led the procession, riding on a great white horse. But Damisa, one of the Nigerians seconded to Gideon Force, had served directly under him. And the Janar had brought him close to tears that night when, as he was leaving, he drifted towards Damisa's table and as he went past said, 'I see the leopard is here,' and continued on his way with, some said, a faint smile in his eyes.

But it was this moment of great pride for Damisa that was to cause the quarrel later that night when the men gathered in his basha.

Banana and Pash were already there with him, as the billet was his as well as theirs, when Farabiti Danja and Farabiti Guntu joined them. Zololo was the last to arrive and the first to speak about what had brought them together there that night.

'By God, that was a marvel tonight, what the Janar did as he was leaving,' Zololo began. 'After all these years he still remembers you. There must have been thousands of you out there in Abyssinia and yet he still remembers Samanja Damisa.'

Damisa tried to play it down. He tried to pretend that it was nothing really. 'People never forget me,' he said with an embarrassed laugh, pointing at the spot at the side of his head where his left ear used to be.

'But he not only remembered you, he remembered your name. That,' said Zololo firmly, 'is something.'

Everyone nodded in agreement. The Janar was indeed a noble lord. Samanja Damisa was indeed a credit to all infantrymen, to the West African Frontier Force, and to the Nigeria Regiment; and all the men felt honoured to serve under him.

The quarrel started when Zololo, noticing what he thought was a look of puzzlement on Kofur Pash's face, turned to the kofur and said in English: 'The janar called the samanja a leopard. Damisa is Hausa for –'

'Leopard,' said Pash lighting up a cigarette. The look on his face wasn't puzzlement at all. He'd merely been searching for his lighter.

'Your Hausa is getting better every day,' Zololo observed, switching back to Hausa.

'So is your Yoruba,' Pash responded in English, his face hidden behind a cloud of smoke.

'Now the kofur is insulting me,' Zololo announced, a dangerous glint entering his eyes. 'The kofur knows I don't speak Yoruba.'

'Cheer up, Dogo,' said Pash in Hausa, calling Zololo by his other name. 'I was only joking. Have a Lucky Strike. And by the way, my name's Fashanu – not Pashanu. It's Fash, not Pash.'

'The kofur's good humour is getting the better of his memory tonight,' said Zololo. 'The kofur forgets that I don't smoke.'

'Well then perhaps you should,' said Pash. 'And I've got some rum as well, if you're feeling thirsty.'

Damisa knew Zololo well enough to know that if he didn't intervene now, the evening could end with a murder. He sprang to his feet, strode across the floor and struck Pash sharply on the cheek.

'What in God's name is the matter with you, Olu?' he shouted.

'I'm tired of Dogo and everyone else making jest of

my Hausa,' he said, his face flushed with rage and stinging from the slap. Pash was known, behind his back, as Kofur One-By-One because of his tendency to mix up words. He would say *d'ai d'ai*, for instance, which means one by one, when he meant to say *daidai*, which means correct. The result was that when he meant to say "You're correct," it came out as "You're one by one." This provided endless amusement for everyone except Pash. He was a very shy eighteen-year-old who couldn't bear ridicule.

'And you think starting a fight with Dogo is the solution?' Damisa asked him.

'I know I speak Hausa with an accent,' Pash began.

'It's not your accent that's the problem. It's your grammar that's appalling,' Zololo kindly pointed out before Damisa told him to shut up.

'I know I make all sorts of mistakes,' Pash conceded. 'But I can't help it. It's not my language. I'm not Hausa. I'm Yoruba.'

'And a good Christian too,' observed Zololo innocently. So innocent, in fact, that he too earned a slap from Damisa.

'What's wrong with calling the man a Christian?' Zololo yelled in protest.

'There's nothing wrong in calling him a Christian,' Damisa agreed. But he knew that what Zololo really meant was that Pash was not a Muslim.

'Then why did you strike me, Samanja?' Zololo seemed genuinely aggrieved.

'Because it's bad manners to remind a man of something he knows only too well,' said Farabiti Guntu, trying to be helpful. 'It's like reminding me that my name is

Guntu.' He had a booming, high-pitched voice which, he proudly claimed, once knocked a fly unconscious when he screamed at it to leave him alone while he was minding his own business and trying to enjoy his mango in peace. Guntu used to eat a lot of mangoes in those days; one year he ate so many that he had to shut down his mango stall in Birnin Kebbi. He'd come to Burma to escape the queues of mango farmers he still owed a lot of money.

Guntu's real name was Dogo, which means the tall one, but Guntu was actually quite a short man. And since Farabiti Zololo, who was tall, was also called Dogo, it was decided that Guntu – whose real name was Dogo – would be called Guntu, which means the short one, and Zololo – who was quite tall – would be called Dogo, to avoid confusion. It was most confusing at first for the short Dogo, but after a while he got used to being called Guntu which wasn't his name at all. But neither was it Dogo. His real name was Guntu but he'd changed it to Dogo when he joined the army to avoid being tracked down by all the farmers whose mangoes he'd eaten.

'Is Private Guntu saying there's something wrong with being a Christian?' Pash demanded.

'Is Kofur One-By-One saying there's something wrong with being short?' Guntu swiftly retorted.

Guntu's outburst was followed by total silence. Then his eyes bulged in realisation and his mouth split open, a horrified orb, and he began to stutter an apology.

But Pash wasn't listening. 'What did you just call me?' His furious eyes bored into Guntu's head.

Guntu looked to Damisa for help but the samanja simply

shrugged. A sigh of misery and resignation ran through Guntu's body. Then his eyes fell on Zololo, who had a smirk on his face, and suddenly he shouted, making everyone jump: 'It was him!' he shouted, wagging an accusing finger at Zololo. 'He was the first to call you Kofur D'ai D'ai. Ask Samanja Damisa. He was there at the time.'

'Sarge?' Pash said. But Damisa refused to get involved.

Slowly, Pash turned and faced Zololo. 'Is it true?' he said quietly. Ominously.

It was at that moment that Danja, who was sitting behind Banana, decided, for no apparent reason, to join the fray.

'But your own name isn't even Guntu,' Danja pointed out. 'Your name is Dogo.'

'If I say my name is Guntu,' said Guntu, turning viciously on Banana, thinking he was the one, 'then Guntu it is.'

'But I didn't say a thing,' Banana protested.

'Now you're calling me a liar as well.' Guntu's voice had become shrill.

'I'm calling you no such thing,' Banana said, cowering away from the onslaught of spittle. 'I didn't say a thing. If you're looking for a fight go and pick on someone your own size.'

As Guntu happened to be the smallest person in the room, he naturally took this to be another insult.

'That's it,' he said, springing to his feet. 'That's more than enough insult for one night. If you'll excuse me, Samanja, I'm going back to my tent.'

'Sit down, Guntu,' Damisa barked at him. Guntu sat down.

'You were all there tonight when the Janar said my name in front of the whole column,' Damisa began. 'He said my name because he's a gracious man. He said my name because he remembered me from Abyssinia. He remembered not just me, but all those thousands of Nigerians, including Dogo here, who fought bravely alongside the two thousand men he had directly under his command in that ferocious war with the Italians. I've heard that the Janar himself personally requested at least one Nigerian brigade when he sat down to plan this coming expedition to Burma. They say he wanted Nigerians because in Somaliland and Abyssinia he saw that we were brave fighters and hard-working men. I do not know if the story is true, but I like to think it is. Consider this: of the six brigades that form the Chindits the only one that's not made up of men from England or Scotland, or made up of Americans, is our very own Thunder, the 3rd West African brigade. Even the Gurkhas do not have a whole brigade to themselves. And the Gurkhas are famed for their bravery and ferocity in battle. D-Section is made up of eight men. Eight men who until not so long ago were farmers, traders, fishermen, tailors and blacksmiths in a far-away land called Nigeria. Now we are sojas all, come to fight King George's war. Now we are in India and, as you heard tonight from the Janar, in less than ten days we'll be in Burma. Back home most of us didn't even know each other. Some of us met for the first time on the ship sailing here or right here in India. Some of us are Christians, some Muslim, and some worship their ancestors. Some of us speak Hausa, some Ibo, some Yoruba, and some Tiv, and some speak other languages. I don't care what God you worship, or what language you speak; I don't care whether you are short or tall or thin or bulky; I don't care whether you can read or write; whether you drink or whether you prefer water. All that matters to me is that you can shoot straight and that you know that we are all brothers now. We stand together or together we die. I mention death because I know that some of us here tonight will not make it back from Burma. This is not a prediction, just a fact of war. Some will go back home without even an itch that needed a scratch on their body. I'd like to think that if I were to die in Burma, someone who was here in this hut tonight will one day, fifty years from now, gather his grandchildren together under a full moon and say to them: I knew a man once, we fought together in the trenches of Burma, his name was Abdul, he was blunt but fair, he was like a brother to me. I knew a man once, he died in Burma.'

A hushed silence descended on the room. A strange mood had taken hold of the men; a feeling, which each man keenly felt and struggled against, of being close to tears. Godiwillin walked in at that moment.

'I see you've all heard the news,' he said, sounding quite numb himself.

'What news, Will?' they asked him.

Godiwillin was called Will, not because his name was William, but because Godiwillin was too much of a mouthful and they refused to call him God because only Godi Almighty answered to that name.

'Haven't you heard? The Janar is dead,' he said. 'His

71

plane crashed less than twenty minutes after he left us tonight. Captain Gillespie told me just now.'

The twin-engine B-25 Mitchell bomber had flown straight into a mountain near Bishenpur at the border between Burma and India and disintegrated on impact, killing all nine people on board.

II

ABERDEEN

1

A few nights after the Janar's death, the valleys of Hailakandi echoed with the ear-splitting chatter of twin-engine planes. As one plane landed, followed by another, eighteen officers together with three hundred and ninety-seven men of other ranks, and fifteen ponies, seventy mules and eighteen bullocks, took their turns to step into them.

A few hours earlier, Kyaftin Gillafsie had gathered all the various groups in his platoon together.

'I've heard talk,' he said in Hausa, 'that we are guerrillas. I've heard even Chindits say so. They should know better. We are guerrillas only to the extent that we are structured in small cells and trained to strike at a moment's notice and, if need be, to vanish immediately without leaving a trace behind. But it is misleading to think of ourselves as guerrillas. We are not guerrillas. We are, in the words of the late Janar Wingate, a Long-Range Penetration group. Brigediya Calvert, C.-in-C. of Emphasis, our brother brigade the 77th, who worked closely with Janar Wingate to plan this campaign, has come up with the most appropriate description of what we are. In the Brigediya's description, the eight columns of Emphasis, and the six of Thunder – the 3rd West African brigade – and those of all the other Chindit brigades – Galahad, Enterprise, Profound and Javelin – not to mention the auxiliary forces, will separately penetrate every type of country, like the outstretched fingers of one's hand spread in every direction, and then concentrate on bringing those fingers to clutch at the enemy's throat when his attention has suitably been scattered, or strike a blow with a clenched fist at an important objective such as a bridge or an ammunitions dump. In other words, men of Thunder, we march divided, but we fight united.'

The men, as one, leapt into the air cheering and shouting repeatedly, 'Thunder! Thunder! Thunder!' and when they dispersed and went back to their huts to finish packing, the tightness that had begun to claw at their insides had gone. It was replaced by a heady feeling of purpose that brought a new spring to their steps.

2

D-Section was in the last batch to leave.

It was dark inside the Dakota. The fuselage reeked of leather and hydraulic fluid. The engines roared, first one, then both, and the runway lights merged into one fleeting copper-tinted blur rushing past as the plane surged forward with a deafening grunt and climbed steeply into the air with a sharp jolt that flung Banana out of his seat. His head slammed into a hard object that turned out to be Farabiti Zololo's ankle. He crawled woozily back to his seat and clutched the metal grip with all his strength.

'Samanja,' he called out in Hausa, trying to sound calm. 'What's the name of this place we're going to in Burma?'

Kyaftin Gillafsie's voice rang out in the darkness.

'It's called White City,' he said, 'that's where we're going.'

Farin Birni, Banana repeated it to himself, White City.

Even the kyaftin sounded excited.

3

That was two nights ago. Two nights only and yet it seemed to Ali Banana, as he now struggled up another hill, that it was such a long time ago. By the light of the moon, he could make out the figure of Danja in front of him. Danja's kit was dragging him down. Now and again he would hitch it up and after a few minutes it would slide down his back.

And was that Will further up the twisting path, or was it Bloken, sneaking a sip from his chagul, even though drinking water on the move was strictly forbidden? No one knew why it was forbidden. Some said it was bad for the stomach, others said it sapped endurance. But there was Godiwillin stealing a sip from his canvas of water.

No, he thought, looking again. It wasn't Will. And it couldn't be Bloken. Somewhere in the back of his mind,

Banana remembered trudging past Bloken – perhaps as long as an hour ago. Bloken had collapsed by the foot of a tree, his face stretched tight with misery. Banana had paused briefly and then, like the men before him and like those after him in the line, he had silently continued along the footpath. Bloken had fallen and there was nothing anyone could do for him. Only Bloken could save himself.

Behind him, Zololo, who had earlier given up, slumped against a rock, and then summoned the energy to continue and had now caught up again with the group, was breathing heavily and cursing, rather loudly, the 'Thik Hai' leading the march. The 'Thik Hai' were the Gurkhas. Thik hai, meaning 'all right' in Hindustani, an acquired tongue for the Nepalese Gurkhas, was their casual and invariable response to every, situation and everything said to them and so the Nigerians started calling them Thik Hai. In their small bodies – they were short and lean – these men possessed the strength of a wild water buffalo. They walked with great, powerful strides, and if you were close enough to observe their feet, it seemed as if one foot sprang forward before the other touched the ground. But very few of the marchers were close enough to the Gurkhas to observe their strides. They had walked at this pace all day, never once flagging, never pausing to catch breath.

There was an even greater distance between the last man in the line and some of those who had collapsed out of sheer exhaustion and could not or would not continue. These stragglers were left behind to fend for themselves. They could not complain; it was understood

– and had been repeatedly stated during the months of training – that during a march it was every man for himself. If every man who fell had to be carried by another man – who could barely walk himself – casualties would multiply. It was known from the first Chindit expedition the previous year that such men as these, who fell and could not continue, often died not from tiredness or starvation but at the hands of Jap patrols. And although they were yet to encounter a Jap, the men on the march knew there were plenty about. The rocks and valleys across which they walked were the rocks and valleys of Haungton, three hundred and twenty kilometres behind the Japanese frontlines in Burma, every inch of it held by the Japanese. It was knowledge of this fact that spurred the men on even when their bodies had all but given up. It was terror of what the Japs would do to them that roused the men who fell and persuaded them to pick themselves off the ground and crawl if need be, until they caught up with the rest.

The fire which earlier had frightened Banana and made him nearly flee had ceased to trouble him. That fire, which wasn't a fire at all, but a million fireflies fused together into one giant piercing flame, had long ago disappeared. But the fear had not left him. He no longer remembered the excitement he'd felt only three days earlier. That feeling was gone, replaced by this numbing, if not disabling, anxiety.

4

This was not how it was meant to be. They had known that there would be walking once they got to Burma, but this particular walk hadn't been part of the plan. Events on the ground had forced it on them.

The flight from Hailakandi had gone without a hitch. And it seemed as if they'd hardly entered the clouds when the plane began its descent. Paddy fields appeared below and soon a river which Kyaftin Gillafsie identified as the Chindwin.

'Hold on tight, boys,' he said. 'White City is here. We're about to touch down.'

The kyaftin spoke too soon, but it was a good thing he'd told them to hold tight. A minute later, barely a kilometre from the ground, the Dakota suddenly lifted its nose and headed straight back up, hurling Gillafsie, who hadn't followed his own advice, and several stray packs, down the fuselage. The plane rose another kilometre before changing course and just as suddenly it began to come down. Ten minutes later, they landed in a valley at a makeshift airstrip surrounded by *taungs*, ancient hills that had dropped, it seemed, out of the sky and crashed onto the edges of other hills. Over the valley and from both sides of the crevice the hills jutted sharply forward, almost, but not quite, meeting in the middle. They hung over the valley like a half-open sunroof.

The airstrip looked like a graveyard of planes and gliders. Everywhere they looked there was a C-47, just like the one that had just spilled them out, with its nose sandwiched between the rocks and its tail dangling in the air, or a glider that had crashed so forcefully it had folded into itself before scattering in all directions.

'Plasma?' a figure in the dark snapped at Bloken, the first one out.

'No, sir,' Bloken replied. 'Bloken Yahimba – Jap killer, sir.'

'Where are we?' asked Jamees Show, a British NCO.

'Aberdeen,' barked the shadowy figure. 'Brought the plasma?'

'What plasma?' asked Samanja Show, but the man had already moved on.

'Plasma? Brought the plasma?' they heard him ask the crew.

'Blood,' Show explained to Bloken. 'He's a medic.'

They'd landed at Aberdeen, Kyaftin Gillafsie told them, because White City had come under heavy bombardment from the Japs earlier that night, shortly before their attempted landing. Five other Dakotas carrying members of their column had been diverted to Aberdeen. They would all stay the night here and make their way on foot to White City at first light.

No one, not even Samanja Damisa, cared to be the one to ask him how far they had to walk from here to get to White City. But Gillafsie knew they were dying to know.

'It's only seventeen miles away,' he told them.

When the kyaftin was out of earshot, Samanja Show laughed grimly.

'It's only seventeen miles away,' he said cheerfully to Banana. 'But there's a little problem, a little mountain of a problem, between.'

Samanja Show had joined them just before the flight in India, arriving at Hailakandi straight off the plane from Nigeria where he'd served as a colour-sergeant, a rank above sergeant. He'd been so keen to join Wingate's Circus that when the call for sergeant volunteers came he'd accepted a demotion and signed up.

'A little whathing, Jamees?' asked Samanja Damisa who was standing further away from Samanja Show. 'Farabiti Ali no speak English. He no understand is what you say.'

'Don't you?' Show asked the farabiti.

'Small-small,' replied Banana. He did understand what the British samanja had said. He just couldn't yet speak the language. He now proceeded to translate what the sergeant had said, quite accurately, into Hausa, adding that he didn't know what it meant.

'You could have fooled me,' Samanja Show said in

Barikanchi – a pidgin form of Hausa spoken in army barracks – and walked off to join his group.

'What did the sergeant say to Banana?' Godiwillin – whose Hausa was good but not quite as good as Bloken's – asked Bloken who was crouched beside him struggling with his kit.

'I think he said there's a problem along the way,' Bloken told him. He hadn't been paying much attention to the conversation.

'What problem is that?' Godiwillin asked anxiously.

'I don't know what the nature of the problem is,' said Bloken, 'but it's on a mountain somewhere.'

'This is no time for jokes,' Godiwillin snapped.

'But, Will, I wasn't joking,' Bloken said seriously. 'I'm telling you what I heard.'

Bloken turned round to say something to him but Godiwillin had already walked away and was now standing beside Zololo and nodding thoughtfully.

'What did Dogo say?' Bloken asked him when he came back to pick up his kit.

'He said get some sleep, it's going to be a clerk of a walk.'

Aberdeen was home to Enterprise, one of their brother brigades. Once they were inside the perimeter fence, everyone hurried to find a slit trench to sleep in. Some reached for a shovel and dug out a hole. A few brave ones, too tired to dig a hole, found shelter in the wrecked Dakotas on the airstrip.

5

Stand-to was at four in the morning. Then, immediately after breakfast, they were on their way, escorted by four Gurkhas who were going to White City anyway, and three Karen scouts, natives of the hills of Burma.

III
TOKYO

1

The going was easy at first. They sauntered through a village and startled a group of girls washing by a stream. The girls smiled shyly and then tore off into the rice fields as soon as the men smiled back.

They stopped at the stream to fill their chaguls. They had been told never to drink from a stream unless an officer, preferably a Medical Officer, had certified the water safe to drink. But as they had no MO with them, Samanja Show filled in for one. At forty, Samanja Show was the oldest man on the march.

A herd of buffaloes was guzzling away downstream.

'If it's good enough for them I reckon it's good enough for us,' Samanja Show declared, which seemed perfectly sound logic.

They passed through another village but, except for

stray dogs, which seemed intent on marching with them, it was eerily quiet, nothing stirred from the teak and bamboo houses. Soon, after a ten-minute water stop, they encountered a second deserted village, its sole occupant a Buddha in a golden pagoda. A rumour travelled through the line that the Karen scouts, also known as Burrifs because they were on loan from the Burma Rifles, who were in front leading with the Gurkhas, had said that a deserted village was a clear sign that the Japanese had recently been there and might still be in the area. It was this rumour more than anything else that started the gradual unravelling of the men. After this, every shrub and every rock concealed a Japanese sniper and every strange sound was a shot aimed at them. Their paranoia was catching and soon even the pi-dogs growled fearfully whenever the men looked to them for reassurance. Eventually, as lowland gave way to rising hills, and the sun emerged in its full ferocity, the dogs simply stopped, gazing dolefully after the men, and went no further.

Banana was used to the sun burning so hot that even the earth on which a man walked scorched his feet and it was as if he was walking on smouldering coal. But the heat of this sun was unlike any that his homeland had ever thrown his way. It wasn't just the heat. It was the utter dryness that got to him. He was walking through the densest forest he'd ever seen and yet not a single leaf fluttered around him. The air was still and there was no breeze.

It didn't help either that he and every other man on the march was saddled with a load on his back. Apart from the chagul filled with half a gallon of water in the haversack hanging from his belt alongside two big pouches loaded with grenades and a Bren magazine, he had, strapped to his back, a 'Himalayan Pack', a rucksack with a frame which contained one spare bush jacket, one spare pair of jungle-green trousers, one pair of rubber hockey boots, four pairs of socks, three pairs of spare laces, a vest, a jersey, one water bottle with two litres of water in it, one small towel, a bar of soap, a toothbrush and nail clippers, one gas cape, one groundsheet, one blanket, one mess tin, a knife, fork and spoon, a drinking mug, water-purification tablets, field dressing and Elastoplast, a housewife sewing-kit, a water-proof wallet for personal letters, one bottle of Mepacrine, some anti-mosquito cream, a mosquito net, a ration bag containing five days' 'K' rations, and two orange handker-chiefs with a map of Burma printed on both sides, which could be worn on the head as an identification signal to friendly aircraft. In addition, he was carrying a rifle, fifty rounds of ammunition, a bayonet, a *kukri* or a matchet and sheath, a toggle rope, an entrenching tool and a clasp knife. Officers and British NCOs also carried a wristwatch, a prismatic compass, binoculars, a torch, as well as maps, pencils and notebooks. Each man was issued with twenty-five silver rupees to be used only in an emergency. In essence, each man was hauling a rucksack weighing over thirty kilograms.

2

As dusk approached, the order came to halt just as fatigue was beginning to take its toll on them. The officers had chosen a site high enough for them to spot intruders approaching in all directions but not so high that a passing Jap bomber would immediately take an interest in them. They were to bivvy here for the night.

For a few minutes they all lay on the grass, flat on their backs, and let the breeze, which had returned now the sun was gone, wash over them. They drank from their chaguls and then settled down to the grim but necessary task of eating their supper. Field Ration, Type K, or the 'K' ration as it was better known, consisting of three meal-packs in one box, was an American invention designed to sustain troops under emergency conditions when no other food was available. It consisted of a fruit bar, a tin of meat and a packet of biscuits which all looked like paper pulp that had been pasted together and tasted like cat food; a pack of purified grape sugar which tasted nothing like grape or sugar and was so revolting even the mules refused to eat it; and a pack of lemonade powder so acidic it worked better as a floor-cleaner than as a drink. Only the pack of four Camel, Lucky Strike or Chesterfield cigarettes that came with the supper pack – considered superior to British Army supply cigarettes and highly prized among the sojas – made the ordeal of 'K' ration worthwhile.

But there were no fires or lights allowed that night and no cigarettes either.

After supper, they formed a square perimeter and installed headquarters, including the signallers, sappers, officers and various specialists who were non-combatants, in the middle. Each man dug a trench and sentries were chosen from each group and posted to the flanks. They slipped into their trenches with the knowledge that they had covered ten miles that day and had only another seven to go.

Most slept through the night, their fear conquered by fatigue, and dreamt of making it to the end of the march. But Banana woke at the slightest sound. It wasn't fear that kept him awake. Just the sheer enormity of finally being in Burma to fight for Kingi Joji. He'd wondered aloud during one of their rest stops what the odds were that sooner or later he would run into Yusufu and Iddrisi, his childhood friends, who were also somewhere out here in Burma. But Damisa had assured him that although it was possible that this would happen, it was also highly unlikely. Damisa used the map of Burma on one of his orange handkerchiefs to show him.

'White City is here,' he said, 'some two hundred miles behind the nearest reaches of the Japanese frontlines and Sixth Brigade are on that hump over there somewhere on the British frontline, our frontline, which is, of course, on the other side of the Japanese frontline. The Chindwin River, over there – we flew over it last night – is the boundary between the two frontlines. For Yusufu and Iddrisi to find you, first they will have to cross the Chindwin which runs from these mountains up north, not that far, but not a short walk from where we are right now. It's a mighty river, the Chindwin. It flows northwest through the Hukawng Valley which is packed with tigers and wild elephants and then south along the Indian border where it joins the great Irrawaddy River in Upper Burma. Having crossed the Chindwin where it meets the Indian border, over there, your friends will then need to cut through the Japanese frontline, which will be quite a feat, and in no time at all – a few hundred miles later – they will be in White City. It's simply unlikely, Ali, that you'll be seeing your friends any time soon.'

3

Either because their bodies were weaker or because the sun was fiercer, on the second day of the march it took the men almost two hours to cover the first mile. More deserted villages crossed their path, and yet another pack of stray dogs adopted and then spurned them. The climbs were steeper and although the hills and valleys of India where they had trained were similar to this terrain, their training didn't seem to make a difference. Or perhaps it did. Perhaps the first man to fall, who fell just after midday, would have fallen much sooner.

A few more rest stops, and longer resting times, would have helped of course. And it would have been nice if Kyaftin Gillafsie hadn't insisted that they had twenty minutes only for lunch instead of the one hour they got the day before.

'There is something afoot,' Pash confidently assured them as he tore open his lunch pack. 'If the captain says that, there is something afoot.'

'And what might it be?' Zololo asked.

'In my hometown we have a saying,' Pash said through a full mouth. 'A man does not run on thorns for nothing: either he's chasing a snake or there's a snake chasing him.'

'Funny you should say that,' said Zololo. 'We have the same saying in my hometown. But we say it a bit differently. A man does not run naked for nothing, we say: either he's chasing a snake or there's a snake chasing him.'

'Maybe you've both got snakes in your hometowns,' Banana said thoughtfully.

'Or maybe they're both running from the same snake,' Damisa said, rising. 'Up and on, fellows. Lunch is over.'

'But we haven't even started yet,' Guntu complained.

'Well,' said Pash, 'you know the story, don't you, about the hungry boy?'

'Which one?' Danja asked.

'A father and his son are walking through the jungle,' said Pash. 'A jungle quite similar to this one. The son says to his father, "I'm hungry, father." "What?!" says the father —'

'"Didn't you just eat two days ago?"' Banana completed it for him.

Pash gave him a mock-curious look.

'Don't tell me you're also from my hometown?' he said with a grin.

'I don't think so,' Banana replied, looking perplexed. 'Everybody in Zaria knows everybody else. I would have remembered your face if I'd seen you before.'

'Maybe he's your long lost brother, Ali,' Danja said to Banana.

'I don't think so,' said Banana.

'Where's your long lost brother then?' Zololo asked.

'I don't know,' Banana said wretchedly.

'How did you know the end of Olu's story?' Guntu asked him.

'He told me the same story when I told him I was hungry an hour ago,' Banana replied.

'I didn't know you had a brother who was lost,' said Damisa.

'I didn't know that either,' Banana said, looking even more confused.

Damisa's eyes narrowed into a bemused squint.

'Are you joking?' he asked Banana.

'Why would I joke about a thing like that, Samanja?' Banana asked, wondering why the others were laughing at him. They'd been laughing at him for days now and he couldn't quite figure out what it was about him that was suddenly so laughable. Only the other night back in Hailakandi, Bloken had told a story about a man who lost a ring inside his house. After looking for some time and not finding it, the man went outside to continue the search. His neighbour asked him what he'd lost.

'"I've lost my ring," said the man.

'"Where did you lose it?" asked the neighbour.

'"Inside the house," said the man.

97

' "Then," said the neighbour, "why are you looking for it outside?"

' "Because," said the man, "there's more light out here." '

The others had burst out laughing and that had puzzled Banana. He waited impatiently for the laughter to die down, then he turned to Bloken and asked, 'So what happened next?'

'What do you mean what happened next?' Bloken said.

'Was it there? Did he find the ring outside his house?'

Banana was utterly baffled by the raucous laughter that greeted his question. He'd only asked because he too had once lost a ring, which belonged to an important customer, when he was still learning to be a blacksmith. Zololo's story had made him wonder if he should have looked for it outside instead of spending all afternoon looking inside the yard where he'd lost it. Perhaps he would still be back home now, no longer an apprentice but working on a good wage for his master who in truth, he thought, hadn't been such a bad man after all. Perhaps if he hadn't lost that ring he wouldn't be out here on his way to a strange land full of people who wanted to kill him.

'Why are you all laughing?' Banana asked as the march continued. He turned to Damisa. 'Samanja, why are they all laughing?'

Damisa shot him a worried look but said nothing. He'd noticed a gradual change come over Banana during the past week or so. Gone was the haughty young man who loved nothing better than the sound of his own voice making long-winded speeches. He seemed instead to have shed the all-knowing mask and become an innocent child of seven. The others had noticed this as well and had taken to making him the unwitting butt of their jokes.

But Damisa had other things to worry about right now. He resisted the temptation to tell Pash that they were indeed pursuing a snake and that the snake might be pursuing them in turn. It was the reason they had had no water stops so far and so little time for lunch.

After stand-to-arms that morning and just before breakfast, Kyaftin Gillafsie had been in touch with Headquarters in India by radio. The signals were erratic because of the hills around them but he'd managed to piece it all together in the end. He learnt that the assault on White City, which had prevented them from landing there the previous night and which had been staunchly repulsed, had been repeated once and again all night long. It seemed it was becoming a siege. But this was no cause for concern. The news from HQ that got him fretful was that a Japanese troop deployment order had been intercepted and if Gillafsie and his men could reach Mawlu by dusk, they would be well placed to welcome a convoy of Jap trucks that should be thereabouts between midnight and three-thirty. Mawlu was a village two kilometres south of White City. More worrying, though, Gillafsie had been told late the previous night that Karen scouts in Aberdeen had sighted a Japanese platoon near one of the villages Gillafsie and his men had passed through. It was fairly likely that the Japs might be on their scent.

Gillafsie was faced with a dilemma: should they stick to the route they had chosen, which would see them in

Mawlu well before dusk and with plenty of time to set an ambush in place, or should they double back and give their pursuers a surprise, or should they continue White City-bound but take a different, possibly safer but longer route? The longer route was only slightly longer, but infinitely more difficult to negotiate. It was parallel to the track they were following, about three kilometres to the east. During Operation Longcloth, the previous Chindit expedition into the guts of the enemy, it had saved many a Chindit's life when the Japanese were hot on his trail. But it had taken its toll in blood. Many who sought its sanctuary were saved from the Japanese but claimed by its rocky warren of treacherous jungle.

Gillafsie held counsel with his group commanders. The Karen scouts were for sticking to their chosen track. They pointed out that if indeed the Japs were behind them, they were at least half-a-day's walk behind, and although the Japanese were fabled for their feats of endurance, the heat which was punishing the Chindits would not spare the Japs either. The Japs fought well in the jungle, it had to be said, but the jungle was also littered with their bones. The Gurkhas agreed but wanted the pace of walking quickened. Samanja Show, who was a group commander, wanted the men told of the situation. It might concentrate their minds, he felt. But there was always some rivalry between the British NCOs and their Nigerian counterparts who, naturally, felt it was better not to. But they had good reason for saying so. Most of their men had yet to be tested in battle, and until a man was tested in battle, no one, not even the man himself, could say whether he would use fear to save his life or lose his life because of fear. News that the Japanese were fast on their heels might well concentrate their minds or it might send the men into panic.

'Balls,' said Show, 'I was in Nigeria for four years. I know these men as well as the next man.'

Kyaftin Gillafsie, who had spent the first seven years of his life in Nigeria, and the next nineteen in and out of it, said nothing.

Gillafsie decided that they should stick to their chosen track, that there should be fewer rest stops, and that the news should be kept from the men. But as a precaution, he also sent one of the scouts back the way they had come to act as a lookout.

4

The lunch stop had been good for the men. They seemed as fresh as when they'd started out from Aberdeen and the jungle was beginning to lose its power to frighten them. They no longer saw a sniper behind every teak, and when a mighty branch suddenly snapped off a tree and came crashing down, they didn't so much as blink.

One man even started whistling and had to be told to shut up. He was whistling Tarzan's trademark cry from *Tarzan the Ape Man* and *Tarzan and His Mate*, both of which he had seen at his local cinema, the Rex, right next to the big market in the Sabon Gari quarter of Kano.

'That was some majigi,' Danja said, wistfully.

'The first one or the second?' Guntu asked.

'I prefer the second. The first one is boring,' declared

Zololo with an air of great authority. He should know; he'd seen the first one twice because he slept through it the first time, and the second one four times because he couldn't get enough of it. And in great detail he went on to talk about these and several other *dodon bango*, evil spirits on the wall, another popular term for the entertainments provided four nights a week at one shilling a ticket at the Rex Cinema. They also talked about their immediate destination, Stronghold White City. Why, Bloken wanted to know, was it called a stronghold?

'It comes from the Bible,' Godiwillin told him. 'From the Book of Zechariah. "Turn you to the stronghold, ye prisoners of hope." That's where the Janar got the idea from.' Raising his voice now, he said. 'The motto of the stronghold is –?'

'No Surrender,' responded several voices.

The stronghold, they'd learnt, was an asylum for wounded Chindits. The stronghold was a magazine of stores. The stronghold was a defended airstrip, an administration centre for loyal inhabitants and an orbit around which columns of the Brigade circulated. The stronghold was also a base for light planes operating with columns on the main objective. The stronghold was, above all, a *machan* overlooking a kid tied up to entice the Japanese tiger. In other words, the stronghold was a red flag raised before a raging bull.

'We wish, firstly, to encounter the enemy in the open and preferably in ambushes laid by us,' the Janar had written in the secret instruction manual used to train the Chindits. 'And secondly to induce him to attack us only in our defended strongholds. Further to make sure of our advantages, and in view of the fact that the enemy will be superior in numbers in our neighbourhood, we shall choose for our stronghold areas inaccessible to wheeled transport. We will impose our will on the enemy.'

The marching men talked about this and that and that or the other. Then gradually, the voices went quiet and all that remained was the sound of men struggling for breath. It was strange how the tiredness crept unawares on them, so that one moment a man felt he could go on marching for ever and then the very next moment he wanted to sit down, just sit down for a few seconds, just a few seconds, Samanja.

Then the sun came out and together with it the heat intensified and it was impossible to breathe and the men started to drop. Fortunately for those like Zololo who dropped and regained the strength to continue, the progress of the march had slowed to little more than a crawl and so he was able to catch up.

Soon after Banana got his fright from the fireflies, he started silently to howl with pain wondering whether he was going to make it. Zololo was mostly quiet now but every so often he would regain his voice and curse the leading Gurkhas with great feeling. Samanja Show was swearing too. Blast, Banana heard him say, blast.

Banana couldn't agree more with the sentiment but he was too weak to join in the cursing. Cursing, in any case, wasn't his style. He heard another voice that sounded familiar and looked up. It was Kyaftin Gillafsie further up in the line, heading towards the rear of the march and going from one man to the next, urging them on. It was the first time Banana had set eyes on the kyaftin since he left his position behind Banana, shortly after the fireflies, and hurried to the front of the march.

Damisa too reappeared. He had left soon after the kyaftin, heading back along the track.

'I'll be back in a while,' he'd whispered to Banana, 'if anyone asks for me, tell them I've stopped to answer nature.'

In fact he was going back for Bloken and Guntu and Danja and the other men who had fallen by the wayside. Too many had dropped and Damisa was convinced he could coax a straggler or two back on their feet. And now he'd returned. Banana didn't ask him how he'd fared. He had returned alone; that said it all.

'What time is it?' Banana asked. 'It must be midnight or later.'

'In Nigeria, yes. Right here in Burma, it's only sixteen hundred hours,' said Samanja Show. 'You're right though. It does feel like midnight – tomorrow.'

'But the moon, Samanja, the moon,' Banana said weakly, pointing up.

'What moon?' asked Zololo, beginning to choke with laughter in spite of everything.

What Banana had mistaken for moonlight was in fact an unseasonable darkening of the skies. The clouds had started gathering shortly before the incident of the blazing fireflies.

Minutes after they spoke a flash of lightning streaked across the hills and as the rain, mighty and thunderous, began to fall, an audible sigh of relief coursed through the line. The march stopped and the men unslung their packs and sat there in the downpour grinning foolishly and as happy as children.

The rain lasted a quarter of an hour, then it slowed to a drizzle, and the sun, still fierce and hot, returned. But the heat didn't matter so much now. And it didn't matter that their packs were now twice as heavy. When the march resumed, their spirits had revived and it showed in the strides they took.

Two hours later, when the village of Mawlu appeared in the distance, every single man who had fallen behind had rejoined the marching platoon.

5

At four in the morning there was still no sign of the Japanese convoy. Ready with rifles, Brens, Mills grenades, and shoulder-fired anti-tank Piat guns, the Chindits lay, knelt, stood and sat in concealed positions along the Mawlu road. The village itself was only a mile away to the north. Behind them a railway line ran parallel to the road. Not a single train had passed since Gillafsie and his men arrived there more than ten hours ago. Even if one did come along behind them, the wild shrubs and trees on the boulders overlooking the road below would keep them all but invisible to the naked eye.

For the ambush, Gillafsie had chosen a point on the road where it climbed up a knoll for about fifty metres from the south and then curved downhill for another fifty metres before furrowing round a sharp bend to the north.

Their target was expected to come from the south but it didn't matter much which direction he came from. Vehicles approaching from either direction would be forced to slow down as they negotiated the slope. Gillafsie had chosen his best men for the killing group. They were placed closest to the anticipated point of contact with the convoy expected. Damisa and Zololo were in this group. Planted at various points higher up and a bit further back was another unit whose job was to provide covering fire for the killing group. This unit was as crucial as the killing group and it was anchored by Samanja Show who was said to be something of a crack shot. Their brief was to open fire only if the enemy started to flee and the killing group were forced to break cover and expose themselves while pursuing the enemy. The muleteers and their mules and two of the signallers stood guard several hundred metres away, hidden behind a fastness of bamboo reeds, keeping watch over the rear with a pre-arranged signal to alert the others if they sighted anything suspicious.

Banana found himself lying next to Aluwong, a boy of about nineteen who was from another group. Aluwong was from Kagoro, a small village of rugged hills near the mining town of Jos. Banana had noticed him a few times back at the base in India but their paths hadn't crossed until now. Between them they had a box of grenades which looked, they both commented, so much like a basket of onions. They were to reach into the box as soon as the killing group opened fire and lob the grenades at anything that looked like enemy still breathing.

The men were under strict orders not to open fire, not

even to make the slightest movement – even if the enemy appeared to be approaching their site of concealment – until a signal from Kyaftin Gillafsie indicated that every man who had a target in his sight should fire. The signal was the single-shot breech-loading Very pistol which, when fired in the air, issued a yellow flare that would briefly illuminate the dark night.

6

After the kyaftin's final briefing to the column and just before they moved into position, D-Section gathered together.

'Don't shoot high,' Damisa said. He was telling them what they already knew, what they'd spent months living and breathing in training. But with the exception of Zololo, they were all children as far as Damisa was concerned. It wouldn't hurt them to be reminded.

'Whatever you do,' he repeated, 'don't shoot high. Choose your target carefully. If someone else closer already has him in his sights, choose another target. Don't all fire at the same target.'

'Unless of course only one Jap shows up,' Danja said. But no one laughed, and after a while his laughter turned to embarrassment.

Guntu wanted the group to pray together, but Damisa said no. There was no time for that.

'Pray on your own,' he said. 'But remember the words of the Prophet, "Trust in God, but tie your camel tight."'

Bloken prayed to the leather-bound amulets strapped round his neck. One rendered him bulletproof. Another made him invisible to enemies. Yet another ensured that he wouldn't miss a shot.

That had been nearly five hours ago and still there was no sign of the enemy.

7

Banana and Aluwong were the first to feel an almost imperceptible tremor from the ground beneath. They listened carefully and heard nothing but the muffled breathing of the men around them. But only moments later they felt the tremor again. They looked at each other and decided to risk a severe telling-off from the commander. Aluwong nudged Banana, indicating the kyaftin's position.

'No,' whispered Banana. 'You tell him.'

But it wasn't because Aluwong was afraid to speak to the kyaftin.

'You're closer to his position,' he whispered fiercely.

Banana could hear his heart pounding loudly as he prepared to speak.

Thinking in Hausa, he raised his voice slightly and

called out to the kyaftin, 'That's them, sir,' and realised with shock that the words that came out of his mouth were in a language he'd thought he didn't understand. The words had come out in English.

At first no one heard anything that bore out Banana's claim. It was nearly three minutes before a faint rumble of engines coming from the south reached their ears. The platoon had been quiet before but now they were so quiet even the buzz of a mosquito flying about seemed almost as loud as the trucks that were gradually approaching. They could hardly breathe but they were calm also, patient even, happy to stay their hands until the kyaftin gave the word.

Soon, a truck appeared on the first hillock and as it slowly descended a second appeared behind it and then a third. The trucks were travelling with no lights and the darkness was so thick it was impossible for the men to see further than a metre away. Each new truck manifested itself by the rumble of its engine and the quarrelsome clatter of its changing gears as it mounted or descended the hills. Japanese voices murmuring quietly and talking loudly vied with the motors for the men's ears. As the first truck crawled towards the northern bend, a fourth appeared at the rear. The firing started the moment the flare burst out of Gillafsie's pistol. In the pitch darkness every man and his gun was now in the killing team. Weapons fired in rapid bursts ripping into metal. The truck at the front and the one bringing up the rear were the first to explode. The night ignited into great balls of flame. Briefly, before the explosion died out, they saw the faces of the men they were killing. Their faces too were lit up by orphaned tongues of flame. Some faces were twisted with the bilious rage of fear.

A wandering bomb soared beyond the trucks and disintegrated into several smaller bombs as it struck a tree like an axe with a thousand blades, carving the thick stem into several pieces and flinging the disembodied upper trunk with its crown of shattered branches into the solid undergrowth behind. The smell of burning rubber and wood and roasting flesh filled their noses. The ambush had lasted no more than five minutes. But it took several more minutes before the noise of small and medium arms and exploding grenades began to die down. Soon the moans and cries coming from the trucks died out too.

It was impossible to tell whether they had got all the Japs. They knew they'd struck all four trucks but the night was so dark it was as if a black wall of steel had grown between them and the road below.

One thing the Brits had learnt from bitter experience was that if there had been any survivors, they would remain within vicinity of the ambush. British sojas, if they survived an ambush, would let their feet do the talking and as quickly as they could manage. The Japanese would do no such thing. Instead, they would duck into the nearest jungle and entrench themselves, waiting for as long as it took for the next Allied soja to come within sight of their rifle, or until they were hunted down.

Gillafsie decided they should wait until daylight before inspecting the damage they'd wrought. There were no howls of celebration, no yells of victory. It wasn't because they felt for the men they'd killed. It was because they were tired. Sleep was all they could think of. They quietly set about forming a perimeter between the railway line and the road. They hacked out slit trenches and even though it was nearly five o'clock, and dawn was almost upon them, those not on sentry duty fell asleep as soon as they crawled into the dug earth.

8

Banana and Aluwong shared a trench, and as he fell into a deep sleep, Banana realised that he couldn't remember Aluwong's name and made a note to ask Damisa first thing in the morning.

Less than an hour later he was rudely awakened by the short, quick bursts of a Bren. Banana sprang like a coil, reaching for his rifle and checking it was loaded, and then he peeped out of the foxhole. Nearly forty other pairs of eyes were peering out of their sockets, wondering what was going on. Loud, furious swearing followed by apologetic laughter came from the eastern flank of the perimeter. Banana retreated into the trench, placing a hand across his forehead to still the sudden ache that was threatening to pierce it.

He didn't find out, and wasn't immediately interested

in what had caused the shooting, until later that morning when he was told that it was the return of Ko Ye, the Karen scout the kyaftin had sent back in the direction of Aberdeen the previous day. Ko Ye had retraced his steps all the way to the stronghold and had found no signs of the Jap platoon he'd gone searching for. Walking alone, but still weighed down by his pack, the trek to Aberdeen and back towards White City had taken him fifteen hours. When he reached the outskirts of Mawlu it had taken Ko Ye a while to find the platoon, but by the time he knew where they were, they were already lying in wait for the convoy. To avoid being mistaken for a Jap and killed by friendly fire, he'd dug a foxhole about a kilometre from them and watched the ambush take place. He'd waited till it was light before approaching the perimeter. The shot they'd heard had issued from the weapon of a tired, over-zealous sentry who hadn't heard him approach. Luckily for Ko Ye, apart from bad nerves and a few scratches sustained when he dived, he was, as the Gurkhas would say, 'Thik hai, Johnny.'

'That's not why Samanja Grace shot him,' Aluwong said to Banana who had heard his version of the story from Godiwillin who heard it from Pash who claimed to have heard it from Ko Ye himself. 'Grace shot him because when he challenged him, Ko couldn't remember the password.'

'Who told you?' Banana asked.

'Grace himself told me. He's my group commander.'

'I heard,' said Guntu, joining them, 'that Grace mistook him for a hostile native because he wasn't wearing his uniform when he appeared at the perimeter. That man has got the lives of a cat. The same thing happened to him at Aberdeen.'

'Who told you?' Aluwong asked him.

'Just now I heard the kyaftin and Samanja Damisa discussing the incident.'

At that moment, Ko appeared in the distance looking, like everyone else, bleary-eyed and worn out. And, like everyone else, he was in uniform.

'He wasn't in uniform when he left yesterday,' said Guntu walking away, looking disapprovingly at Ko's British army uniform as if the man had personally let him down.

'How many of them are in there?' Aluwong asked. They were standing at the edge of the perimeter looking down at the trucks piled one upon the other, riddled with huge holes and full of bodies.

'Samanja Damisa counted thirty-five pairs of boots. Some were blown up from the waist up, but every one of them still had his boots on.'

'Poor bastards. I wonder what's going to happen to their boots.'

'We're going to burn them up together with their boots when the mop-up team returns from the bush with the other bodies.'

'Samanja Damisa said some of them wore gold teeth,' Banana said, looking at the intertwined bodies below.

'What was he doing searching the mouth of a dead man? What was he hoping to find there?'

'He went down there with ten men. They were searching

for things that might be useful to Intelligence Section in India.'

'How did they know what to look for?'

'They don't. They simply collect everything, notebooks and diaries especially, and pack them off to Intelligence. One of them was wearing a Samurai sword.'

'What's that?'

'It's a sword,' Banana explained with a big yawn. He turned to Aluwong. 'Do you think we killed any of them?'

For a moment Aluwong looked confused. Then he said, 'With the finafurs you mean?'

The grooved cast-iron Mills grenades looked exactly like pineapples.

'Yes. Did our finafurs get any of them?'

'I don't know,' said Aluwong rubbing his eyes. 'I simply pulled the pins and threw them as quickly as I could. I was too terrified to look.'

'It's strange what those finafurs can do,' said Banana after a long silence, hiding his hands as they started to shake.

'This place reminds me of my home town,' said Aluwong. 'The rocks, the bamboo, the cactus. It all reminds me of Kagoro. I wouldn't be surprised if they grew mangoes here as well. God, I could do with a mango right now.'

'I could do with a whole day of sleep.'

'Me as well. That's the first thing I'm going to do when we get to White City. I'm going to dig myself a nice, big hole in the ground, spread out my groundsheet and stretch out like a prince.'

'I know. You already told me once yesterday,' said Banana. 'And I was going to ask the samanja when I saw him just now so I didn't have to ask you again but I forgot. The samanja, you see —'

'Which samanja?'

'Samanja Damisa. He never forgets a name. Tell me, Aluwong, what's your name?' *Sunan ka ya bace mini,* he said, your name's slipped my memory.

Banana's hands had stopped shaking. He waited for Aluwong to answer his question, but Aluwong simply stared at him. Then Banana realised why he hadn't answered him: 'Aluwong, of course,' said Banana.

'That's funny,' said Aluwong. He thought about it and said again, 'That's very funny.' He didn't laugh though. He was too tired and the effort would have been too much. But he did think it was funny, although he couldn't say why.

'You won't believe what strange things have been happening to me recently,' Banana said. 'During the march yesterday, for instance, when we came across those fire-flies —'

But Aluwong's mind had moved on to other things and he wasn't listening to Banana.

'I forgot to take my Mepacrine yesterday —' he began.

He didn't finish the sentence. A barrage of Brens, rifle shots, grenade explosions and Japanese light machine guns burst out from the jungle across the road. As they fell flat on their stomachs, with stray bullets flying past their heads, Banana turned to Aluwong to ask him if he thought the Japanese weapon firing so feverishly was the ferocious

Nambu they'd been told to watch out for and even taught to fire. Aluwong lay motionless, the right side of his face buried in the grass, his eyes open wide with a look of mild surprise, a hole on his forehead spurting with blood and dripping with bits of his brain. The bullets were still whistling around them. Flat on his stomach, Banana slid away from the perimeter, his face glued to the earth as he clawed his way back to the safety of his slit trench.

9

He had barely entered the hole when he heard Damisa's voice barking out to him. 'Come on, Ali,' he said. 'The mop-up team needs back-up.'

Banana couldn't pretend not to have heard. The samanja was staring down at him, completely unaware, it seemed, of the shells whizzing around.

Aluwong's body was still lying where he'd fallen. Someone had draped a groundsheet over him.

'Bring your matchet with you,' said Damisa, looking grimly at Aluwong but saying nothing. 'It may come in useful. And your bayonet as well.'

'Hankali,' Samanja Show called out after them. Be careful.

A few minutes later Banana and five other men followed the samanja across the road. They held their hands to their noses and hurried past the trucks. It was eerily quiet. The shooting had stopped.

They walked past a teak tree bearing a sign freshly carved into it:

TOKYO 2972 MILES

At the edge of the jungle, they ran into Zololo and Bloken supporting a limping Pash between them.

'Jap got me on the knee with a Nambu,' he said apologetically. 'It's just a scrape though. Dogo nailed him before he could do serious damage.'

He insisted that he could walk back to the perimeter by himself. He tried to stand on his own but keeled over. Bloken pulled out a flask of rum and pressed it to Pash's lips. Pash's eyes lit up as soon as he took a sip. It was just the tonic a man needed, he said, inhaling a lungful of smoke from the cigarette Zololo now placed between his lips.

'If a man gets fussed over this much just because he's suffered a scratch on his knee,' he said, 'I just might go back in there and ask Jap for more.' The rum had done him a world of good. Hanging onto the shoulder of a Gurkha, Pash headed back toward the perimeter, his face shining with sweat and delight.

'Kofur One-by-One,' Zololo called after him.

'Yes, Dogo?' Pash answered, turning round.

'Be kind to that knee. Don't walk so fast,' Zololo said.

It was obvious to them all that, despite his claims to the contrary, Pash was in a great deal of pain.

'The whole bush was crawling with Jap,' said Zololo

as they entered the forest. 'But I think we've got most of them now.'

The firing started again about two hundred yards to the west. Then it stopped. 'That must be Danja and Will. I'll go and see that they are all right. You go right on. Grace is over there to the right with Samanja Ko and the Thik Hai.'

Zololo headed west, followed by Bloken. They turned east and had barely walked fifty yards when they ran into Grace and the Gurkhas.

'Man pass man, no man pass God. Opportunity come but once,' this was Grace, thumping his chest.

'All neighbours be cousin to rich man, but poor man's brother does not know him,' he declared.

But he wasn't quite finished yet.

'Beware of expensive ladies,' he solemnly advised. 'Always remember dat no condition who permanent. Opportunity lost but once. Good advice is poor food to a family dat hungry. Beware of harlots and many friends. Never trust all dat love you. Money hard for get but easy for spend. Ambition is di last refuge of failure. Corner-corner love is no love at all. Trouble does not ring bell.'

He did a warriors' dance, his razor-sharp *adda* dripping with fresh blood.

The Gurkhas stared at him in utter amazement.

'There were three of them,' said one of the Gurkhas whose *kukri* also bore the soaking evidence of fresh use. 'Is it all right to leave their bodies here? Grace said the captain wanted them all brought back to the truck.'

'It makes no difference where they are. Kyaftin just wants to know how many there are,' Damisa told the Gurkha in a tortured mixture of broken English, Hindustani and Gurkhali.

They heard Zololo's voice coming from the other side of the bush. They heard Danja's voice too. Zololo was laughing at something Danja had said. Shut up, you crazy fools, Banana screamed in his head, scared the samanja might decide to send him to go and find out what it was that was amusing them. But the chatter and Zololo's laughter seemed only to reassure Damisa that everything was under control. He said they could go back now to the perimeter with the Gurkhas and Grace. It was nearly nine o'clock and Kyaftin Gillafsie wanted to make White City before midday.

Ko said the Japs were devious bastards. They all wanted to die, he said, but not before they'd killed you first. The only way to make sure they were dead, even after you'd shot them, was to stick your bayonet through them. Samanja Grace kept apologising to Ko Ye for almost killing him. Banana remembered Aluwong had said Grace was his group commander. He wondered if he'd heard about Aluwong. He was about to tell him the news as they were emerging from the undergrowth and on to the road when they heard a quick series of great explosions behind them, followed by an anguished scream. When they came out from behind the trees where they had taken cover, they saw a black apparition staggering towards them. It was Bloken. His face and uniform were covered in blood and scraps of flesh. Seconds later, Danja and Godiwillin appeared behind him. They too were splattered with blood.

'Where is Dogo?' Damisa asked them.

'Dogo is dead, sarge,' said Bloken.

Damisa blinked, looking slightly confused. 'But I heard him laughing just now,' he said.

'Dogo is dead,' Bloken repeated, sweeping a piece of flesh off his hairless head.

'If he's dead,' Damisa said, 'where's his body?'

'There was nothing left to bring,' Godiwillin said. 'We were walking past a dead Jap – we thought the bastard was dead – when he suddenly blew up. The wretched son-of-a-clerk must have had several grenades on him. He must have seen us coming and pulled all the pins and pressed himself flat on the grenades. Dogo had just stepped over him when it all went off and we all dived. When we looked up there was nothing left of Jap. And there was nothing left of Dogo.'

Wearily, Damisa leant against a tree. He was only twenty-six; in Banana's eyes he'd always behaved like a man of twice his age. But now as he rested his head against the teak tree, he looked like a little boy lost.

'Go on,' he said to them, 'I need a moment alone. I need to think.'

As they slowly walked away, he called out to them.

'Bloken,' he said, 'how's your head?'

'My head is all right,' said Bloken. 'I'm just shaken, that's all. I'll be all right once I've had a wash.'

'We're heading off to White City within the hour,' Damisa said to them. 'Bloken and Pash are not to carry any luggage. Split their kits among the section. Don't look so alarmed, boys. White City is just around the corner. An hour's walk at the most.'

'But I can carry my own pack, Samanja,' Bloken protested.

'I know you can,' said Damisa. 'But I think you are concussed. You need to take it easy until the medics take a look at you when we get to the stronghold. You, Ali, go fetch the flame-thrower. Tell Guntu to give you a hand. We need to burn those bodies in the trucks before we leave.'

Banana turned to go fetch the flame-thrower, but Damisa's voice stopped him in his tracks.

'Tell Guntu to give you a hand,' the samanja told him again. Then he seemed to remember something else. 'Pash's knee looked quite bad,' he said, looking at Danja and Godiwillin. 'He'll need a pair of crutches made for him.' Then his gaze returned to Banana. 'Forget about the flame-thrower,' he said. 'Samanja Show and his group are going to take care of the dead Janpani. Go and find a spot within the perimeter and dig a grave for Aluwong. Tell Guntu to give you a hand.'

After the samanja had finished speaking, Banana turned to Grace waiting for his reaction to the news of Aluwong's death. But Grace's face registered nothing. He was still in the grips of a dazed exhilaration.

They left Damisa there and headed back for the perimeter. Grace, gradually coming back to earth, said it had been a long march and the sooner they got to White City the better. He said it in pidgin and the Gurkhas

127

didn't understand him. Ko Ye said he'd heard the sound of heavy fighting that morning coming from the direction of White City. Bloken had a searing headache and couldn't really say much.

Samanja Grace was still going on about looking forward to getting to White City when he suddenly stopped, a cloud rising across his face, and grabbed Banana by the neck.

'What does Aluwong need a grave for?' he asked in Hausa. It was obvious that Damisa's last instruction to Banana had only now sunk in.

'You're strangling me, Samanja,' Banana said, gasping for air.

'Sorry, Farabiti. I didn't mean to.' Grace let go of Banana and then, in a quiet voice, he asked: 'Where is he?'

'In the perimeter, sir,' Banana said, 'I'm sorry, Samanja. I was going to tell you.'

But Grace didn't hear him. He was already running towards the perimeter.

The others said nothing and didn't change their pace of walking. Banana thought he saw some vultures hovering overhead but he was becoming wary of seeing things that weren't there so he turned to Bloken and asked, 'Are those vultures up there?'

'Yes,' said a voice behind them, 'they clear up the mess.'

It was Damisa. He'd caught up with them.

'I went back and found this,' he said, 'now at least we've got something to bury.'

He held up a helmet with a hole as big as a fist in it. For one moment, when the samanja held the blackened helmet up against the morning sun, Banana thought it had all been a bad dream and he'd now woken up and Zololo was there with them walking back to the perimeter, and soon together they would reach White City.

'Dogo,' he gasped. 'I thought you were dead.'

'I am, I am,' said Zololo rather impatiently. 'What's that in Damisa's hands?'

'Your helmet,' said Banana. 'Don't you recognise it?'

'That's not my helmet,' answered Zololo. 'Tell him it's not mine.'

'Whose helmet is it if it isn't yours?'

'The Jap's.'

'Where's your helmet then?'

'It's right here on my head,' said Zololo. And it was. Farabiti Zololo's helmet was right there on his head.

'Ali,' called someone behind him.

He turned round to see Aluwong sidling up to him.

'What's Samanja Grace doing over there?' Aluwong asked.

'He's digging your grave,' Banana told him.

'Oh,' said Aluwong without further interest.

They stopped by the Tokyo sign.

'Tokyo or home, Dogo?' Aluwong asked Zololo.

'Home,' said Zololo.

'Why not Tokyo, Dogo?'

'Jap son-of-a-clerk probably doesn't want to see us, don't you think?'

'I guess you're right, Dogo. But I've always wanted to go to Tokyo. I've always wanted to go to Tokyo and New York. Next time maybe. Let's go home, Dogo.'

There were no tearful goodbyes; simply a brisk, smart salute and then they were off, marching back toward Aberdeen, a two-man brigade, yodelling like a football stadium:

> *Ai remembah when ai was a soja,*
> *Ai remembah when ai was a soja,*
> *Ai remembah when ai was a soja,*
> *Ai remembah when ai was a soja.*
>
> *Hippee ya ya hippee hippee ya-ya,*
> *Hippee ya ya hippee hippee ya-ya,*
> *Hippee ya ya hippee hippee ya-ya,*
> *Hippee ya ya hippee hippee ya-ya.*

Banana watched them for a long time, singing silently with them. He returned their salute as their backs receded in the distance, wondering whether he should tell the samanja what Zololo had said about the helmet. He decided not to. When he looked round, he found he was alone. The others must have left him when they saw him talking to Zololo and Aluwong.

He crossed the road, covering his nose as he went past the trucks. He passed Samanja Show who was heading the other way, a flame-thrower strapped to his back.

Inside the perimeter, Grace was still digging Aluwong's grave. Banana quickened his pace. He wanted to take one last look at Aluwong before the earth covered him.

IV

WHITE CITY

1

White City emerged from a thin mist of grey dots which revealed themselves, as they drew closer, to be canopies of white parachutes fluttering above the giant trees spread across a square kilometre of spiralling hills and sunken valleys overlooking a wide stretch of open paddy fields and dark, green forest. A tall wall of concertina wire marked the garrison's boundaries.

White City was by no means impregnable, but anyone attempting to enter the simple fortification uninvited could reasonably assume that he would be dead even before he made it past the dannert wire wound round it. Laid out liberally at all approaches to the block were mines and anti-personnel bullets designed to enter a man's body through his foot before departing through his head. If the booby traps didn't get the intruder, the grim-faced sojas manning the wires would see to it that their Brens and Stens did. Behind the sentries stood powerful Bofors guns and Howitzers loaded and aimed in every direction, their crews changed every twelve hours, always at the ready for the slightest sign of trouble.

A telephone network routed under the trenches, bunkers and dugouts sprawled all over the block, and a new invention, the portable, bi-directional radio transceiver called the walkie-talkie, provided a steady line of communication between the multiple strands of the garrison's defence mechanism.

'That's how White City got its name,' Samanja Show told Banana, pointing at the parachutes. 'Each of those chutes is a supply drop that didn't quite make it past the trees. Most of them got snagged there on the night this stretch of jungle became a stronghold. At first our boys thought it was a simple matter of climbing the trees and cutting them loose. But they quickly learnt how unwise that was. Every other sod who went up got plucked down by a Jap sniper. So they stopped trying to retrieve the chutes and White City, which came from the pilots, became its given name. It's a nice touch – there's a place in London famous for greyhound racing called White City.'

'What were they going to call it before that?' Banana yawned.

'The four other strongholds are named after famous places. Chowringhee is named after a street in Calcutta. Broadway is named after a place in New York. Piccadilly is in London's West End. And Aberdeen got its name from the city in Scotland where the Janar's family comes from. I'm not sure what they were going to call White City, but there actually wasn't meant to be a stronghold here. If you look to your left you'll see a rail track. White City is planted right in its path. Trains used to run along this track twenty-four hours a day carrying supplies from Rangoon to the Japanese troops further north. Now they can't. White City was established to do just that. That's why the Janpani are in such a huff. The ones we sent scurrying to the Maker this morning were reinforcements for those already barraging White City night and day.'

'White City is a great name,' said Danja. 'But Argungu would have been much better.'

'Is that where you're from?'

'By the grace of God, Samanja.'

'I had quite a time there last year during the fishing festival.'

'Why, Samanja! May I divorce if I wasn't there too. I was one of those three thousand fishermen. Why didn't you call out to me? I would have introduced you to my wife's legendary cooking – *tuwon shinkafa* and *miyan kuka* with the tastiest catfish you've ever eaten.'

'Ah, ground rice and dried baobab leaf stew,' said Samanja Show with a nostalgic sigh. 'And catfish. That would have been a treat, Danja. But only a week ago I didn't even know you.'

'That is true, Samanja. But it's no excuse.'

Scores of wary-eyed patrol units glared dispassionately at them from the perimeter. The gateway into the stronghold was a twisted basket of barbed wire that opened directly at the point where the rail track abruptly hit a wall of sand-bags. They squeezed through it one at a time, praying the Japs didn't choose that moment to launch another air strike.

Their prayer was answered, but the last of them had scarcely squeezed through the wire when a voice shouted, 'Take cover!' Followed seconds later by another voice calling out, 'Dakota,' meaning that the first call was a false alarm. It meant there was a plane coming, but it wasn't an enemy plane.

The Dakota now appeared above them but it didn't land.

'It's a bloody tow-truck,' someone muttered. The Dakota had been towing a glider.

Minutes after the C–47 disappeared, the Waco glider, which had hitched a ride behind it and then unhitched itself as they approached White City, now appeared. The glider banked towards the airstrip on the western ridge of the stronghold. Suddenly the glider plunged into the dense thicket of trees on the hill below. It didn't crash to the ground but emerged from the trees seconds later, completely redesigned; its wings were gone, neatly and completely plucked off. It was quite clear now that it was going to crash. But again, it didn't. As it came diving toward the ground its cockpit and nose suddenly jerked up into the air, as if a thousand giants inside the fuselage had been hurled to the back of the plane. A bulldozer the size of an adolescent bush elephant fell out of the Waco and came hurtling to the ground. Having success-fully finished the business of giving birth, the glider crashed back into the wild green forest. Minutes later, the crew gingerly crawled out of the wreckage. A heavily bearded South Staffords soja got into the bulldozer and switched on the engine. It grunted to life.

2

Kofur Olu Fashanu's war was over two hours after the column arrived at White City. The medics at the dressing station situated next door to Brigade HQ at the centre of the stronghold took one look at his shattered knee and told him it was back to India for him. Instead of showing gratitude, Pash burst into angry tears and insisted he wasn't leaving; all he needed was a rest and his knee would heal itself in no time at all. The doctors gave him a shot of morphia and carried him on a stretcher into a light plane that had come to evacuate casualties.

D-Section flocked to the airstrip to bid him farewell. The kofur was beyond consolation.

'I'm sorry,' he kept saying, as each came to give him a hug.

He sobbed like a child. Just before the plane took Pash

away, Kyaftin Gillafsie came rushing out of the bamboo hut above the bunker that served as Brigade HQ. Gillafsie yanked off the two stripes on Pash's sleeve and replaced them with three point-down chevrons. Samanja Pash's sobs grew louder. He was still sobbing when the plane heaved into the air and headed for Hailakandi. He promised he would be back as soon as he was mended but they all knew he would not. The medics hadn't told him this, but they'd told Kyaftin Gillafsie that Pash's leg would have to be chopped off from the knee down as soon as he landed in India.

Afterwards D-Section drifted languidly towards Muddy River on the south side. Telephones and walkie-talkies cackled incessantly all around them. Several crews were assembling six additional Bofors guns and four 25-pounders brought in the previous night by twenty-five Dakotas amidst heavy Japanese shelling. A floater company of Leicesters sent out to harass the enemy returned with ten men fewer than had left a few hours earlier. But for every Brit that had died, the Japs had lost ten of their men. A company of Lancashire Fusiliers floated out to blow up a Japanese ammunition reserve dump at Indaw, fifteen kilometres away.

3

Never in his life had Banana seen so many bearded men gathered together in one place. As D-Section wandered quietly towards the waterpoint, they went past their brand new bedrooms, a warren of trenches they had dug for themselves on arrival a couple of hours earlier. Their beds were made up of groundsheets and tarpaulin and assorted odds and ends they'd liberated from the numerous glider wrecks that lay scattered all over the stronghold. For roofs, the men laid railway sleepers across the trenches and covered them with parachute silk to shelter them from the sun. They then covered these with shovels of dirt so that anyone looking down from a plane in the sky would see nothing but undisturbed earth. They secured a window to the outside world, and enough room to lean on the parapet and position their weapons by leaving just a bit of the roof uncovered. This also served as the door into and out of their bedrooms on OP Hill, their new home on the far southern end of the garrison.

Observation Post Hill got the name during the first days of the stronghold when the Chindits discovered that its great height afforded them a clear view of Mawlu on their Barr & Stroud binoculars. Pagoda Hill lay to the west of OP Hill. It was called Pagoda Hill because it used to be a Jap base. When the Japs were flushed out of it, they left a little Shinto shrine behind. To the east lay Bare Hill, completely denuded of trees. To the north, at the foot of Dummy Hill – which got its name from the fake airstrip sited there to keep the Japs busy – lay Muddy River.

The stream was crowded with mules, ponies and men when they got to it. Samanja Show and Samanja Grace and their sections were already there.

'Whatever you do, don't drink the water,' Samanja Show warned them.

'Why not?' asked Guntu. He was dying for a drink.

Show pointed to a prominently displayed sign by the bank.

'What does it say?' Guntu asked. He could manage on his own in Ajami, the Hausa-Arabic script he'd learnt as a child. But the Roman alphabet was completely beyond him.

Godiwillin read it out. The sign declared:

WARNING
DEAD JAPS IN MUDDY RIVER
ALL WATER MUST BE CHLORINATED

Muddy River, Samanja Show explained, got its name not because it was muddy but because the water in it was unsafe to drink.

Guntu said he could manage perfectly well without a wash.

'There's no stream in this world,' Danja grunted derisively, 'that hasn't got a body in it.' He plunged into the water.

He stayed under for so long someone nervously joked that D-Section had lost its third member in one day. Moments later, Danja emerged grinning from ear to ear. It was the first proper swim the fisherman had had in a long time.

4

Guntu had a disconcerting encounter with a Jap by the stream that afternoon. Having decided that he wasn't going to venture into Muddy River because of the corpses in it, he wandered off a few metres away and sat at the foot of a young leafy tree to smoke a cigarette. As he took the first heavenly puff and leaned against the tree, he fell flat on his back and sat up to find the tree flying past the security wire and disappearing into the jungle. In its hurry to depart, the tree stepped on a mine and was blown up. Guntu cut short his cigarette break and fled back to the stream in case the other trees suddenly developed feet as well. From that moment on – and for the rest of his life – Guntu would never trust another tree.

On their way back to their underground quarters on OP Hill the men went past Fort Reno, a large dugout roofed with railway steel and covered with sandbags. Fort Reno was the mules' stable.

They had barely returned to their trenches and had hardly settled down to a well-earned rest when they heard a powerful eruption coming from the direction of Mawlu.

'Take cover!' shouted a voice on a megaphone.

Everybody sank into the ground, faces buried into the earth, trying to make themselves as small as possible. The rocket-propelled spin-stabilised projectile roared for several seemingly endless seconds as it raged in a high ballistic arc across the jungle to reach them. It grew angrier and louder and scarier as it approached. The 6-inch mortar bomb exploded somewhere behind them, amidst the trees next to the Dakota landing strip. So powerful were its splinters, several trees toppled over as if a giant saw had sliced through them. Another followed immediately after. Then another.

The coal scuttle, as this heavy-mortar bomb came to be known, was the most fearsome weapon the Chindits had yet encountered in the Jap box of tricks. It had the annoying habit of exploding before the vibrating noise of its arrival could be heard and quite often even before the sojas had had time to take cover.

White City responded with a battery of periscope-fitted quick-fire 25-pounders capable of discharging five rounds of steel-cased high explosives every minute and guaranteed to shred a man to bits from twelve kilometres away.

As the coal scuttle and other high-velocity Japanese mortar bombs wheezed and chortled before shattering behind, ahead, to the east and to the west of D-Section, or right under their noses, the terror which had gripped Banana began to vanish. The muscles in his chest relaxed and he started to breathe again. Death, he realised, would come when it would come. He could only hope that God hadn't yet decided that his time was up. The faces around him were all covered in dust, stones and debris; raw flesh – man, mule and pony flesh – had travelled through the air, sailed with ease through their roofs and landed on them.

Godiwillin had a gash on his arm where a stray piece of steel the size of a .38 calibre bullet, a fragment from the burst metal shell case of the Japanese mortar, had sawn across it like a cutthroat razor before sinking into the wall above his head.

Bloken, whose faith in the amulets strung around his neck was unshakeable, looked serene and unruffled. At one point during the hairiest moments of the bombing the shells were falling in twos and threes and in clusters of four. To everyone's astonishment Bloken chose that moment to break cover and raise his head above the parapet. He then calmly proceeded to give them a vivid report on the Armageddon going on above them. He was only persuaded to return to cover when Damisa threatened to knock him out.

During a lull in the shelling Damisa examined Godiwillin's gash. It wasn't as bad as it looked.

'But that,' said Guntu, digging the shrapnel out of the wall, 'was a really close call, Will.'

'I was born in Onitsha on 6 April 1925,' said Godiwillin, looking straight ahead, his eyes tired but blank. 'A week later, at Holy Trinity Cathedral, I was baptised Godwilling

Lucky Nnamdi. My middle name is Lucky. I am nineteen years old today. I will not die on my birthday.'

A mortar shell landed just metres away from their hideout, sending Banana's insides scrambling to his brain.

To celebrate Godiwillin's birthday, Bloken lit a cigarette and passed it on. Even Banana, who had never smoked a cigarette in his life, took a grateful puff. Then they all turned to the celebrant.

'Happy birthday, Will,' said Damisa.

'Happy birthday, Will,' said Bloken.

'Happy birthday, Will,' said Danja.

'Happy birthday, Will,' said Guntu.

Banana was next in line to wish him happy birthday. But his voice was drowned out by yet another blast.

5

The caustic exchange between the British bombs and the Japanese shells continued without let for over an hour. Then, when it appeared to be over, when the men began to emerge from their trenches, the air-raid siren screeched and they all dived back into their holes.

Wings gleaming with red ensigns, six Mitsubishi Zeros, the legendary carrier-based war stallions of the Imperial Japanese navy, appeared high above the block. They flew in perfect formation. One after the other the Zeros dropped their bombs in a relay that began near OP Hill, across Bare Hill, past Fort Reno, over Dummy Hill and ended right by Muddy River. The falling bombs were accompanied by the blunt rat-a-tat-tat of the medium machine guns aimed from the Zeros' wings and cowlings at the ground below.

Three Bofors autocannons sprang into action. The Bofors crews were more successful in their aim than the Zero bombardiers. Three Zeros shuddered as they were hit. None of the Japanese bombs scored a direct hit on the bunkers and trenches but one Dakota sitting on the ground was damaged beyond repair. A crater the depth of a bathtub and the length of a swimming pool opened up where the razor wire used to be near Dummy Hill.

The Zeros were awe-inspiring but they hadn't quite changed the history of White City, nor had they altered its geography that much. All it took the sappers was ten minutes and a roll of concertina wire to plug the gap they'd created. What the Zeros achieved by simply being there at treetop level for those few seconds was to kill two men and three mules, to maim a few men, to scare several into wanting to crawl back into the shelter of the womb and never to come out again, to make many never want to see another war and to so infuriate some that they became, without even knowing it at the time, men whose whole existence had meaning only when they killed or were killed while trying to kill.

There was silence, broken only by the cries of the dying wounded, long after the bombers were gone. It was nearly dusk by now. Pitch darkness would soon arrive and so too, if they stayed true to habit, would the Japs.

Damisa suggested that they might as well take the lull to catch up on some sleep. For everyone except Bloken, who had brought his amulets, muttered a shaken Guntu, but had forgotten to bring his brains along, it was the most terrifying day they had ever seen. Even Damisa, who thought he'd seen it all, had to admit that nothing in the East African Campaign had prepared him for such unrelenting terror.

They all felt grateful to be inside the trenches. In this frightening place called Burma, to be lying huddled in a stinking hole in the ground on a bed that looked like a coffin felt just like being inside a palace.

Banana stretched out on his groundsheet and shut his eyes, feeling if not exactly like a prince, then at least grateful to be alive. Minutes later, he sprang up with a start, awakened by a loud explosion coming from the jungle behind him. A Jap's body was found there the next morning with a hole in his small-legged, thin-shouldered body stretching from his left foot to the back of his head.

'I can't sleep either,' Damisa's voice said in the dark. 'Want some tea? I've just boiled a kettle.'

'I'd be grateful for some tea, Samanja,' Banana said. He reached inside his haversack for his tin cup and groped his way through the dark along the wall, stepping across several snoring bodies to reach the samanja. As he sat down beside Damisa and gratefully sipped his tea, he noticed that the samanja had the burnt-out helmet from the ambush in his hands.

'Aren't you going to bury that, Samanja?' he asked.

'No,' Damisa replied. Then after a short silence, he added, 'It's not Dogo's helmet. I only noticed it had a sun on it when I gave it a second look after I picked it up. No, it's not Dogo's helmet. Dogo's helmet wouldn't have a sun on it. I'm keeping it as a keepsake of the ambush and of the day Dogo died.'

'How long did you know him?'

'Dogo? We met on our first day as apprentices of the executioner at the Native Authority prison in Sokoto. It was 1930, the year you were born. Dogo was eleven years old. I was a year older.'

The two boys were both *Almajirai* – pupils at *allo* schools, derelict open-air madrasahs where the children of the poor were sent to learn the Qur'an by heart. The pupils, often numbering in the hundreds, lived in the squalor of a house provided for them by their mallam, an imam who wielded his authority with a cowhide switch. In return for board and tuition, the pupils went out in small groups into the community to beg for food for themselves and money for their master.

'By pure chance,' said Damisa, 'my mallam and Dogo's had both come to the conclusion on the very same day that our begging skills left much too much to be desired. We were not bringing in enough to justify our upkeep. So they both hit on the idea of sending us to work with the executioner who had put word out that he was in need of assistants. We did not know this at the time, and nor did the executioner, but we started our apprenticeship on the very day the last public execution took place in Sokoto. Three men condemned for murder by the Sultan's court were led out from the prison into the marketplace where they were shown to everybody before their date with destiny. The method of execution was the stroke of a sword. The condemned man was made to get on his knees with his hands fastened behind him and his neck stretched out. Usually, when there was only one man to be executed, the executioner's assistants would distract the condemned man by walking in front of him and drawing a sword. The executioner, who would be standing behind him, would then step forward and strike off his head while he was still contemplating the sword in front of him. On this occasion however, there were three men and that method could not be used. The condemned men were made to kneel in a row and wait for their turn. They were all young. The oldest of them was not a day older than thirty. And they showed no fear whatsoever. They simply stared into the distance and calmly waited. Our master the executioner was a powerfully built man. He was stripped to the waist and holding the sword with both hands. He stepped forward by the side of the first man and struck off his head with a single blow. The crowd made a moaning sound but the two remaining men remained impassive. The executioner stepped forward beside the second man and again with a single stroke removed the man's head. Again the crowd moaned softly but the third man remained motionless. My master stepped forward and his sword came swinging down for the third time but it missed the man's neck and landed between his shoulder and his back. Blood gushed out as the executioner pulled out his sword and the crowd stopped breathing for a moment, but the condemned man showed no fear or pain. Instead he turned his head and looked at my master from head to foot. "Why," he said reproachfully, "you ought to be able to do better than that." My master apologised with great sincerity. He did not miss the second time. That was the day I met Dogo. And we quickly became friends. So close were we, a few years later, we both got married on the same day. My first daughter and his first son were born within days of each other. We joined the army on the same day. It wouldn't surprise me if God has willed it that we should both die on the same —'

The last word was lost in the powerful explosion which now rocked OP Hill. The Japanese were back and they had chosen the southern flank as their first point of attack. The sleeping men of D-Section woke up with a start and reached for their Sten submachine guns and filled their pockets full with grenades. Each man stood out against the parapet and cautiously took a reading of the situation. At first they could see nothing but a dizzying constellation of burning fragments of mortar bombs and artillery fire. Two Zeros zoomed across the jungle a few hundred metres outside the block perimeter, dropping bombs which in turn set off the hundreds of mines that had been carefully planted there.

A few minutes later about fifty figures emerged from the jungle and charged, screaming as they hurled themselves against the wires. They were all wielding Bangalore torpedoes, an explosive charge placed at the end of a tube, which they detonated as they hit the wires, hoping to breach the block's fortifications. They were killed instantly, either by the explosives or by the great deluge of bullets that greeted them from inside the block. This tactical innovation came from the same war strategists who had invented the kamikaze. The Bangalore torpedo suicide teams succeeded in their mission: a sizeable breach appeared in the wire and hundreds of Japs, preceded by a dozen coal scuttles which sent all heads withdrawing straight back into their trenches, rushed out of the jungle and poured into the stronghold, firing light–machine guns and tossing grenades in all directions.

Thirteen Vickers, one of them operated by Samanja Show and his section, and thousands of Stens, Brens and Mills rained death on the Japs and sent survivors dashing back into the jungle. D-Section had many of them in its sights and picked them off with efficient ease. Banana focused on a Jap his own size and filled his back and head with lead. He watched the man topple over in a heap and die.

The smell of cordite filled the air.

Hundreds of parachute flare mortars, each capable of burning for several minutes with the intensity of tens of thousands of candles, lit up the jungle around White City so that night suddenly turned to day and everything that was seen moving was despatched under a hail of gunfire. Guntu in particular was on the watch out for any trees that looked even remotely like a human being. He fatally wounded two Japs and killed ten trees that night.

Two American P-51 Mustangs came from Broadway to give White City a hand. From a great height, the P-51s repeatedly shelled the enemy positions. The Mustangs had just returned from strafing a Jap airfield where they'd wiped out ten Zeros in one fell swoop. They had a couple of parafragmentation bombs left over from that mission. As a special *sayonara* they ejected the parafrags on the Japs as they headed back to base, wiping out hundreds of the enemy and creating a hole in the jungle that looked as if it had been made by a meteorite.

That shut the Japs up for nearly an hour. But they did return. This time the suicide team impaled themselves on the wires near Muddy River and blew open a corridor there. Again they were vigorously repulsed and driven back into the jungle. They came two more times that night, attacking at one point simultaneously from the OP Hill wire breach and the Muddy River perimeter breach. White City went into hysterical overdrive and unleashed seven batteries of Bofors anti-aircraft guns on the intruders. An unfortunate Zero sent on a mission to blow up the anti-personnel mines by Pagoda Hill found itself answering to nearly 50 Bofors guns all barking at it at the same time. The Zero exploded in mid-air and plunged into the jungle less than 500 metres away from the block. It was so finely fragmented that the biggest piece of the snub-nosed bomber found the following morning was no bigger than a paperback book. There was nothing left of the crew; it was as if they'd been vaporised.

Finally, just before dawn, the Japs gave up the fight and headed back to their garrison in Mawlu. But the explosions didn't cease. The floater companies sent out the day before had set up an elaborate web of ambushes for the worn-out Japanese sojas going back to base. Practically everywhere General Tojo's forces headed within a two-kilometre radius turned out to conceal a most unpleasant surprise.

Fifteen Chindits died that night. Nearly three hundred Japanese sojas perished.

6

If Muddy River had been unsafe for drinking before, it was now practically useless for anyone but vultures. Hundreds of bloated Japanese bodies, part of the convoy that had breached the Dummy Hill perimeters, floated on its surface as far as the eye could see. Before it could be ringed off and declared totally out of bounds for the inhabitants of White City, however, the job of wading through the water and searching the pale disfigured corpses for material that might be of use to Special Intelligence had to be carried out.

This unpleasant task fell to a group that included Samanja Grace's section. Wearing thick rubber gloves and masks, the unhappy sojas diligently went to work. It took them practically half the day and they did retrieve a treasure trove of maps, letters and a wire, probably never sent, from the local Japanese commander begging General Headquarters for reinforcements.

Shortly after midday, as D-Section were putting the final touches to the new fences where the wire had been breached near OP Hill, a call went out on the telephone and radio networks for Samanja Graceworthy Zuma to report at once to Brigade HQ. Samanja Grace never did report to Brigade HQ and he was declared missing later that afternoon, together with two other Nigerians – a kofur and a farabiti – who had been working with him.

Guntu immediately declared that the men had been abducted by the trees. He went straight to Kyaftin Gillafsie and expanded on his thesis. Gillafsie, who had had less than two hours' sleep in three days, eyed him quietly before asking him if he'd forgotten to take his Mepacrine during the past week. Guntu replied, truthfully, that he hadn't. Gillafsie asked him if he was partial to alkwan. Guntu replied politely but angrily that although he did enjoy the occasional tipple, he hadn't been near alkwan since the night before the column left India for White City. Gillafsie told him he wasn't accusing him of anything; he was merely offering him a drink. The kyaftin reached into his pack and brought out a half-full bottle of Johnnie Walker. He poured a snifter of the potent Scottish alkwan into two glasses – one for himself and one for Guntu. They drank to each other's health and then Gillafsie dismissed the farabiti, ordering him to try and catch some sleep before the Japs came calling again that night.

By the time the Japs returned that evening, all the breaches from the previous night had been sealed, the wounded had been evacuated, dead Chindits buried, damaged bunkers repaired, and mines and booby traps re-erected.

An incident that happened while Bloken was working with a company of Gurkhas, replanting the antipersonnel bullets, reinforced his conviction that his talismans would protect him not only from enemy atrocity but from friendly fire too.

The incident happened near Pagoda Hill. One of the sappers, probably out of fatigue, tripped over a booby trap ignition wire which they themselves had just planted. The man, who was at the back of the mining team, with Bloken directly in front of him, lost his right foot in the explosion that followed. The rest of the team, safely out of harm's way, could do nothing to help. The explosion set off another mine planted too close to the first one and Bloken suddenly found himself standing inside a mine field, with antipersonnel devices going off all around him and he completely unharmed. What saved him was a feeling of overwhelming contempt for the stupid little devils that had dared to go off while he, the invincible Jelome 'Bloken Bottles' Yahimba, was still standing in their midst. To show the niggardly bombs, the silly bomblets and the foolish fragmentation devices his displeasure Bloken stood absolutely motionless and glared haughtily at them. He was saved because he stood still.

Afterwards, when he recounted the incident to D-Section, even Guntu, who had been rattled more than anyone else by Bloken's antics the previous day, eyed him with new respect. It was the first time, Guntu remarked, that he'd heard of a man being saved from death by the sheer completeness of his stupidity. He meant this as a compliment. He said it without irony. He said it as if stupidity was the new religion that he, Guntu, desperately wanted to follow. Especially now that trees had taken not only to walking but also to kidnapping human beings.

Like every other member of D-Section, Guntu had arrived in Burma thoroughly armed with powerful amulets. Guntu's amulets, which he wore around his ankle, were made up of inscriptions from the Holy Qur'an sealed inside threaded beads. Guntu was at a loss as to why Bloken's heathen amulets – which, as everyone knew, were completely useless – should fill him with such reckless confidence. One of Guntu's amulets contained the entire ninety secret names of God and yet the Japs were still turning into trees behind his back. It had him greatly worried.

Guntu was a frightened man. He was running scared. He was so frightened he almost killed himself that afternoon. It wasn't a suicide attempt; merely a case of mistaken identity. It happened shortly after he left Kyaftin Gillafsie's trench. The wonderful whisky had warmed his insides and sent him scurrying to answer nature at one of the many pit latrines that were to be found scattered all over the fringes of the block. He'd finished and was heading back to the trenches when someone tried to jump him as he walked past a tree. He ducked and then reached into his pocket and grabbed the first thing that came to hand, which turned out to be a Mills. He pulled the pin, flung the grenade at his assailant and dived for cover as it exploded. A minute later, he sprang to his feet and began to comb the bushes for the remains of the enemy he'd just killed in self-defence. But except for traces of the fragmented bomb there was nothing to be found. There was no one there but himself. Or that was what he thought – until a sixth sense told him to swing round. He swung round and found his assailant trying to duck behind him. He reached for his service pistol and fired repeatedly at the Jap. The other Chindits, drawn to the scene by the sound of the grenade going off, waited until Guntu had emptied his cartridge before they flung themselves on him and overpowered him. When the medics at the dressing station asked him why he'd been trying to kill his own shadow, Guntu stared at them as if they'd all gone mad. Why in God's name would he do such a thing, he asked? They gently pointed out to him that he was found firing at his own shadow.

'I wasn't shooting at my own shadow,' he informed them. 'I was trying to kill a Jap who'd turned himself into my shadow.'

'Really?' they said.

'Really,' he replied. 'Yesterday I saw with my own eyes a tree suddenly turn into a Jap. What am I to do if these Japs keep turning themselves into all sorts of things? I have to protect myself. I don't want to end up like poor Samanja Grace and those two boys who were kidnapped this morning, probably by Japs in the guise of trees or even shadows.'

The medics ran a quick test on Guntu and pronounced him to be in remarkably good health. They decided he was either a practical joker or pretending to be mad so he would be invalided and sent back to India. They gave him a placebo shot in the arm for nerves and sent him marching back to OP Hill.

The injection did wonders for Guntu's spirits that afternoon but he'd neither been joking nor had he been looking for an excuse to get sent off. He'd seen that Jap and the bastard had been camouflaged as his shadow. He'd only taken repossession of his shadow after he'd pumped gunpowder into it. He suspected that the Jap had slipped into his shadow while he was busy answering nature. From that moment onwards, and for the rest of his life, Guntu would take a crap at night only if he was far away from any light source and during the day only when he could keep an eye on his shadow.

Bloken thought Guntu had lost his mind. Why else would the short man keep on calling him stupid for being invincible? He whispered this to Damisa because he didn't want to get into a row with Guntu. Damisa declared that until Guntu started whimpering like a rabid dog, jumping to any such conclusion about his mental health would be rash. He wouldn't say whether he thought Bloken was stupid or invincible or both. But he promised to knock him out with the butt of his rifle if he ever tried that stunt he pulled yesterday again. A soja, he declared, was a great deal more useful invincible than dead.

Danja thought it was unfair of the Japs to have died in such great numbers at Muddy River. He'd so much looked forward to taking a daily swim, the only luxury that White City provided, but now that simple pleasure had been taken away from him by the bloating corpses. It just wasn't fair.

Banana said Kingi Joji had appeared to him in a dream and told him the war was over. Kingi Joji looked like the Janar but was dressed in the flowing garb of the Emir of Zaria. Banana was quite upset when he woke up from the dream and found that Kingi Joji had lied to him. With a twinkle in his eye, Danja comforted him with the assurance that he'd in fact had the same dream. In Danja's dream it was the Emir of Zaria who had appeared to him and told him that the war was over. The emir was dressed in the flowing garb of Kingi Joji. He too was upset when he woke up and found that the emir had lied to him. He started laughing when he said this, which greatly upset Banana. What's happened to the world, Banana yelled, when kings and emirs can no longer be trusted to tell the truth?

Godiwillin, who hadn't been able to sleep since he almost got killed on his birthday the previous day, told them to please, please keep the noise down.

7

That night the coal scuttles returned with such ferocity they left White City's Operational Command momentarily stunned. Then the Zeros weighed in. Then, in two separate formations, the Bangalore torpedo suicide squads arrived. One formation lunged itself against the wires by Muddy River and opened a crack at a cost of fifty Japanese lives. While the British guns were focused on repulsing the swarm of Japs who poured in like water through this gaping hole in the block's northern flank, five hundred metres away the other suicide squad lunged at the wires at the foot of Bare Hill. They created a massive doorway into which came not one but two light armoured tanks with their turrets spitting in all directions. In less than five minutes the tanks claimed more Chindit lives at White City than the Japs had so far claimed since the siege began.

What made the tank incursion doubly galling was that they were British tanks captured by the Japs two years earlier when the then unbeatable Japanese army had chased the Brits out of Burma. The tanks were eventually forced to retreat under a barrage of antitank fire. Fighting went on all through the night, stopping just before dawn.

The tanks returned again the following night, but the block was prepared for them this time. During the daytime break in fighting, the sappers had done a recce of all feasible tank approaches to the stronghold and then carefully planted several huge pressure-operated blast mines at those points close to the wires.

The circular, steel-cased antitank mine, which couldn't be set off by any but the most colossal of human beings stepping on it, was armed by rotating an arming switch which sat on top of the iron-made cylindrical fuse attached by a copper cover to its pressure plate. When a tank rolled over the mine, it pushed the pressure plate hard on the firing pin sitting beneath the pressure plate. The firing pin struck the detonator underneath it, which then fired a booster charge under the fuse, much like firing a bullet into a powder keg, triggering the main charge. Unlike its antipersonnel cousin whose shrapnel was often designed to fragment into thousands of bullets on detonation, the antitank monster would rise like a punch and penetrate the armour of its target before exploding into a million flying sledgehammers. This bomb and several others buried all round the block were the welcome team awaiting the tanks when they came calling the following evening.

To make sure that the ubiquitous Zeros didn't set them

off with their crude but effective mine-clearing method of simply dropping bombs on the mined fields from a great height, White City's ack-ack bulldogs kept vigil all day long depriving the Japanese bombers access to the sky over and in the vicinity of the block. This had the unintended but welcome effect of forcing the Japs to resort to clearing the antipersonnel ordnance sited a safe distance away from the antitank hardware with the lives of dozens of their men; suicide squads clearing the path for suicide squads. It also meant that the block's Piat antitank crews knew exactly where to position themselves when the tanks finally rolled in, as they did shortly after the vanguard suicide formations were blown up.

Immediately after the first tank rolled over its nemesis and was blown apart, a dozen spigot mortars cruised through the night air and rammed home on the second tank. When the Piats were finished with the tanks what remained of them and their crews was not a pretty sight. But this was war and when the shimmering lights of the parachute flare mortars revealed the ghastly wrecks into which the tanks had been reduced, a great roar of joy that could be heard as far as Mawlu arose from White City.

The siege continued in this manner, every day from dusk till dawn, for weeks.

8

A week after Samanja Grace and the kofur and farabiti disappeared, White City got a whiff of where the missing sojas might be. It was around two in the morning. The suicide teams had been to the block and onwards from there to the sweet hereafter; another Zero had been plucked from the sky by flak; earlier that night a laftana with the Leicesters had suddenly collapsed and died with no apparent cause. Close examination of his remains later revealed that a bullet had lodged itself in his stomach by way of the opening at the lower end of his alimentary canal.

In other words, it had been a night just like any other in White City; the dead were dead and those alive were either wounded or well but desperately in need of sleep and a good home-cooked meal.

A major Jap attack had just been forcefully answered and

neutralised. The Jap guns had gone all coy and D-Section were hoping to get an early night, when suddenly, out of the jungle, a Japanese voice called out.

'Black man!' rang the voice. 'The white man is no friend of yours. The white man is your oppressor. Why are you dying for him? Leave him now. Let him fight his own war by himself.'

There was nothing unusual about the Japs hurling invective at their enemies in White City. They did so every other night and were answered in equally colourful language. What startled D-Section that night was that the Japs were speaking to them not in English but in perfectly accentless, unhesitant, impeccable Hausa.

Once they got over their initial shock, Danja was the first to respond.

'*Uwar ka!*' he yelled. Your mother. He followed this up by hurling a Mills grenade at them.

Seconds later, the same Jap voice responded.

'*Uban ka!*' said the Jap. Your father. A Kiska grenade followed seconds later. It landed and exploded, as all the others would, too far away to do any damage.

'*Buran uban ka!*' yelled Guntu. Your father's penis. Then he tossed a Mills into the jungle beyond the wire.

'*Durin uwar ka!*' replied the Jap. Your mother's vagina. This was followed seconds later by a Kiska.

'*Na ci uwar ka!*' shouted Banana. I fucked your mother. Then he sent a Mills flying at the Japs.

'*Uban ka dan Daudu ne!*' responded the Jap. Your father's an effeminate homosexual. Then a Kiska sailed into the block.

'*Uwar ka kifi ce!*' yelled Bloken. Your mother's a dyke. Then he tossed a Mills.

'*Bakin kuturu!*' shouted the Jap. Black leper. This stunned Bloken into such a rage he had to be restrained from scaling the parapet and going after the Jap.

'*Haba jaki,*' yelled Banana to the Jap. '*Ai kai ma ka wu ce gona da iri.*' Now you've gone too far, you ass.

'Blaady facker,' Bloken muttered. 'Blaady madafacker.'

'That's enough,' Damisa told his men. Samanja Show and Kyaftin Gillafsie had heard the saucy exchange from their trenches and crawled over to D-Section.

'Three of my brothers are missing,' Damisa shouted to the Jap. 'Are they with you?'

'I've no use for you or your brothers,' replied the Jap. 'You are of no use to me dead or alive.'

'Those men are good people,' yelled Damisa. 'In God's name, please, tell me if they are alive.'

'Every fault is laid at the door of the hyena,' responded the Jap. 'But it doesn't steal a bale of cloth. I kill men, I don't steal them.'

'That's a great proverb,' said Gillafsie joining in. 'Where did you learn to speak Hausa so well?'

'I wasn't talking to you, white bastard,' the Jap roared back in English, ending the chat with a flurry of Kiskas.

They never heard from the Hausa-speaking Jap again; Samanja Grace's fate remained for ever a mystery.

Guntu declared that he'd been vindicated. Samanja Grace had been abducted by Japs disguised as trees.

'As shadows you mean,' said Bloken with a chortle.

But Banana couldn't help but agree with Guntu.

'Samanja Grace must be with those infidels,' Banana said. 'Who else could have taught the heathens to speak Hausa?'

Damisa shook his head in disagreement.

'That man couldn't have learnt to speak so well in just a week,' said Damisa. 'He certainly couldn't have learnt to speak Hausa from Grace. If he did then he's a wizard because he's learnt to speak the language better than his teacher. Grace's Hausa isn't as good as that.'

Grace was a Gwari man and tended to get his tenses mixed up.

'But how did she know there were Hausa sojas here?' asked Godiwillin, who tended to get his pronouns mixed up when speaking Hausa. The lady he was referring to was the Jap soja who hadn't sounded like a lady at all.

'The Japs may have intercepted some of our communication,' the kyaftin told them. 'There's a great school in London called the School of Oriental Studies where many languages from all over the world are taught. The shehu who wrote the first Hausa kamus teaches there. That's probably where the Jap learnt Hausa. Until the war started there were many Japanese studying in England.'

Banana knew what a shehu was. A shehu was a very wise mallam who had read lots and lots of books. But he didn't know what a kamus was.

'A kamus,' said Danja when Banana asked him, 'is a big book which tells you the meaning of words.'

'Why do you need a book to tell you the meaning of words? Why can't you just ask someone?'

'I guess it's so you don't have to ask anyone.'

'But I like talking to people.'

'Yes, but supposing the person you ask doesn't know?'

'Then,' said Banana, 'I'll ask someone else.'

'Well then a kamus isn't for you.'

'How does it work?'

'A kamus? Simple. To check, for instance, for the meaning of a kamus in a kamus you simply look under the letter *k*.'

'Why is that?' Banana looked baffled.

'Because if you looked under the letter *j* or the letter *l*,' Danja patiently explained, 'you wouldn't find kamus there.'

'Why not?' asked Banana.

'Because kamus begins with a *k*,' Danja declared in exasperation.

'What about shehu?'

'Shehu begins with a *sh*.' The letter *sh* was the twenty-third letter in the Hausa alphabet. 'To look for the meaning of shehu you look under the letter *sh*.'

'I know what a shehu is,' Banana said.

'Well then,' said Danja. 'You don't need a kamus.'

While Danja and Banana were quietly chattering away, the conversation had moved on from Samanja Grace and the Hausa-speaking Jap. Kyaftin Gillafsie was telling them about how devout the Janar had been and how this devoutness sometimes caused misunderstandings with some of the sojas who served under him and who were themselves not at all that devout.

'Shortly before he died,' said Gillafsie, 'the Janar went to visit the Cameronians – the Scottish Rifles – a few days before they flew in to Chowringhee. As always with Janar Wingate, he liked to talk to his men. He liked to gather round the fire with them and talk to them. "I've got good news for you and bad news," he said to the Scotsmen. "The bad news is: you will be outnumbered by Tojo's army in Burma. The good news is: you will defeat them." "Ah should hope so, sir," said a kofur, eyeing the Janar's helmet quizzically. "We are all agents in the trade of war," said the Janar. "The enemy sells fear and misery. We bring hope and salvation. In Burma you will be propagating the bottomless mercy of God." The kofur's eyes glazed over when the Janar said this. He'd always assumed that he was going to Burma to fight for king and country. "In Burma," the Janar continued, "you will be the agents of God's wrath on Tojo's evil empire. You will triumph in Burma because you will be armed with the greatest weapon ever invented, the most potent weapon ever known to man." "And what would that be, sir?" asked the kofur. "You'll be armed," replied the Janar, "with the sword of justice and protected by the Breastplate of Righteousness. If God is for you who can be against you? Some of you may not make it back. Some of you will remain on the paths and on the hills of Burma fertilising the soil. But that is the nature of war. How does that strike you, soja?" the Janar said to the kofur. "Aye, well," said the Scotsman. "You and God can fucking well do it without me, sir." '

Even Banana, who was slightly alarmed that anyone would say such a thing about God, found the story amusing. After the non-stop hell of the past week though, he well appreciated the Cameronian's feelings.

'On another occasion,' said Kyaftin Gillafsie, 'during the first Chindit campaign, the Janar and the column he was leading ran out of food. They'd been on the run from the Japs for two weeks and had found it too risky to call for supply drops. When they finally shook the Japs off their tail, the Janar got on the radio to Brigade HQ and said, "Oh Lord, give us this day manna from heaven." The radio operator at Brigade HQ paused to work out what the Janar meant. Then he replied, "The Lord hath heard thy prayer." And a few hours later, a Dakota flew past the column's bivvy and dropped a parachute. The chute contained sixty loaves of bread.'

After he'd stopped laughing along with everyone else, Banana turned to Danja and asked him what manna from heaven was and if the Janar and his men had run out of food why did Brigade HQ send them just sixty loaves of bread? Had HQ run out of 'K' rations? Danja said he didn't know. All he knew was that the story must be funny if the kyaftin and everyone else thought it was funny.

'I've heard rumours,' said Samanja Show to Kyaftin Gillafsie, 'that any day now White City will be evacuated and abandoned.'

'Does that mean we're going back to India?' Godiwillin's face lit up.

'Not bloody likely,' replied the kyaftin. 'The primary reason we're here is to rattle the Japs. Now we've done that in White City, Janar Lentaigne may decide it's time to move the parade to another setting. But that won't be in India. It'll be right here, in another corner of this fucking jungle. I've heard talk of plans to create a stronghold further up north. I hear it's going to be called Blackpool. That's probably where we're headed next. I've even heard some crazy talk that we might be disbanded and sent to join the Americans in China. But right now it's all just talk. Until Janar Lentaigne decides, no one knows what's going to happen to us.'

Janar Lentaigne had been named commander-in-chief of the Chindits after Janar Wingate's death. No one knew Janar Lentaigne because, unlike Wingate, he never visited his troops on the field. He never gathered around a fire to chat with them. Some said it was because he hated flying. Others pointed out that Wingate hated flying too but he still flew out to meet his men because he knew it showed he cared. Where Janar Wingate had led from the front, his successor led by remote control. They said the new commander-in-chief refused to come out to see them because he hated Janar Wingate and that, although he was a Chindit himself, Janar Lentaigne thought the Chindits were a waste of time. Some said the reason the brass had given the post to Lentaigne instead of the other janars who were more in tune with Wingate's thinking was precisely because now Wingate was gone, the paper pushers at GHQ in India, who hated, reviled and feared Wingate when he was alive, were bent on destroying his brainchild. Lentaigne, they said, was an administrator who had been sent in to strip the assets of a business no longer considered a going concern.

The conspiracy theorists, amongst whom were virtually all the best Chindit commanders, backed their claim by pointing out that when news of Wingate's death reached

India, the universal reaction in the corridors of GHQ was an outbreak of celebration. The Chindits' paranoia would be vindicated after the war when even the official army chroniclers of Wingate's career would go out of their way to belittle the role the Janar had played in the Burma Campaign. Wingate's reputation would remain under a cloud. Only the translation – a decade later – into English of the memoirs of the Japanese generals who fought against him would begin to rescue his name.

Account after account by members of the *Gunreibo Socho*, the Imperial Japanese Navy General Staff, would reveal that the psychological impact of having the Chindits, whose numbers they vastly overestimated, harrying them right there in their own backyard had had far reaching consequences. It shattered the myth, which they themselves believed, that the Japanese were unassailable in the jungle. The Japanese had conquered the jungle not because the jungle favoured them above everyone else but because it favoured the brave and the Japanese were breathtakingly brave and singularly audacious. And they knew this.

This was why it came as a complete shock to them when confronted by an off-key intelligence whose tactics not only baffled them, it often made a mockery of their boldest moves. In the wider context of the Burma theatre, what Wingate's troops did to their bodies amounted to little more than a scratch on the nose; what he did to their minds was an altogether different matter. Wingate's brazen stratagems wrong-footed the Japanese commanders into making some of the worst tactical blunders that eventually cost them the war in Burma.

'I've heard all manner of talk,' said Gillafsie. 'But as the Janar himself would have said, it's all furofaganda. Everything is furofaganda.'

The Chindits were in serious trouble. Their worst enemies were no longer the Japanese. With the Janar's death, they had become orphans. They had become a nuisance, a pack of stray dogs let loose in the jungle. They were out here killing and being killed on a campaign that their commanders in India viewed with as much hostility as their Japanese adversaries.

These unhappy thoughts were gnawing at Gillafsie's mind, but he wasn't about to voice them to his men.

'Right now,' he said smiling grimly, 'we've got Jap outside the wire trying to kill us. Our job is to deny him that pleasure. Our job is to kill him at every opportunity. And that's exactly what we're going to do.'

He reached into his pocket and brought out a flask of rum. Everyone else who drank pulled out their ration of spirits. Damisa and Banana raised their tea cups.

'Here's a toast to the dead already,' said Gillafsie. 'And here's to the next man to die.'

Immediately after the toast, Bloken started singing, quietly at first then at the top of his voice as everyone responded to his call.

'*Home again,*' he called out.

'Home again,' the others responded.

'*Home again,*' he called out again.

'Home again,' they responded.

'*O my father.*'

'Home again.'

'*O my mother.*'
'Home again.'
Then all together they sang:
When shall ai see my home?
When shall ai see my native land?
Ai will never forget my home.

Their voices must have roused the Japs from their slumber. Seconds after they started singing, they heard the signature thump of a coal scuttle and the monumental shriek of ten thousand fragments of steel as the mortar shattered above them.

'Jap furofaganda,' Bloken said.

'That's all it is, Bloken,' Gillafsie nodded, swallowing another gulp of rum. 'Let's see how they like ours.'

They reached for their Brens.

9

One morning, a few weeks later, seven heavily armed men lifted the dannert wire and quietly slipped out of White City. They trod with caution. Three days earlier one of their own, a man whose name they didn't know because they didn't know him when he was alive, had died. The nameless man, a sapper who knew this minefield as intimately as a grape-grower knows the soil of his farm had taken a step to the right instead of to the left – or was it to the left instead of to the right? – in the grisly vineyard of death surrounding the stronghold. He was blown to pieces by the fruits of the vine he himself had planted.

Ko Ye strode ahead of everyone else in the widely spaced single file procession. Between him and Damisa, who brought up the rear, were Godiwillin, Guntu, Danja, Banana and Gillafsie. With the exception of Banana whose face seemed to grow more baby-like by the day, a moon-like face that didn't need a shave because there was nothing on it to shave, the men's faces hadn't seen a shave in months.

Damisa reminded Banana of descriptions of Shehu Usman dan Fodio, the Sufi scholar who only a century earlier had founded the largest nation state in Africa around the banner of a Jihad.

Gillafsie looked like the much-married Henry VIII.

If Long John Silver, the pirate, or Hernando Cortés, the Spanish Conquistador, had wandered out of the mists of history or from the realms of fantasy and descended upon the hills of Burma that morning they would have encountered men sporting beards not unlike their own.

The pious and sober-making mujahid and the much-divorced king and the one-legged quartermaster and the governor-general of the New Spain of the Ocean Sea would have noticed that these thin, undernourished apparitions looked remarkably sanguine that morning as they walked under the dappled sunshine streaking down on them from the swollen branches of the tall, tightly clustered trees towering above like the fluttering masts of a ship.

The bearded sojas were on their way to relieve a floater company who had radioed for reinforcements after a blood-soaked skirmish at Nyaunggaing, a village some ten kilometres away.

Each man wore a badge depicting the Chinthé, a beast with the body of a lion, the head of an eagle, the teeth of a dragon, the ears of a donkey and a snake for its tail. The Chinthé, guardian symbol of the Buddhist pagodas of Burma, could pounce on an enemy from nine different positions all in one strike.

As on all Chindit marches, none of the men wore any indication of rank or status on their camouflage battle-dress.

Salutes were forbidden; snipers had been known to use a salute to identify officers as prime targets.

Every single inch of the journey from White City to Maiganga – as Banana called it – was fraught with peril. Barely two hours after they set out they almost walked into a company of Japanese sojas making their way towards them. They had so little time to hide, if they had extended their hands they could have touched the Japs' feet from the thicket into which they dived. As each man lay crouched, counting the feet marching past him, his heart-beat went completely loopy as he fought the temptation to open fire. Each man knew that this thought must also be going through the minds of the other men, and they all knew it would be sheer suicide if any one of them gave in to the burning urge. It was one thing to spring a carefully planned ambush; quite another for seven men to take on nearly three hundred on the spur of the moment.

After that near disaster, they avoided the footpath altogether and navigated a slightly longer route through the jungle.

Apart from the ever present heat which fell upon them at noon and turned the jungle into a baker's oven, and the glare of the sun which struck like knives at them, the journey felt almost like a holiday.

10

It was certainly a holiday from the prison of White City. Over the past several weeks, as the Japanese attacks became merely another nightly inconvenience, the stronghold had turned into a purgatory riddled with death and disease and it had become so foul-smelling that being inside the block, or anywhere near it, was like being trapped inside an airtight canister filled with methane.

The smell emanated not only from the men, who had ceased washing themselves since Muddy River became a floating morgue; it came not only from the dead mules scattered all over the block; it came not just from the epidemic of flatulence that had worked its way through every second man in the block; it came most of all and with pungent, unrelenting force from the decomposing bodies of nearly two thousand Japs strung in an endless array of morbid contortions on the concertina wire encircling the stronghold.

So strong was the smell that pilots flying into White City now found their way to the stronghold by the putrid stench that hit their noses while they were still miles away.

Ten thousand vultures descended on the wires every morning and reluctantly left in the evening only when the first coal scuttles arrived and they knew that the men were about to embark once more on the strange ritual that never failed to replenish their avidly consumed food supply. The bald-headed scavengers grew so lazy they would often not leave the ground once they arrived at the caravanserai in the morning and until the mortars obliged them to depart at night. In a feverish orgy they would gorge themselves, emitting piercingly loud rasping squawks of appreciation, and then collapse on the ground for a contented nap, after which they would rouse themselves with great difficulty and once more tuck in to the feast of dead and decaying flesh. The birds grew so fat their necks disappeared into their chins.

Along with the vultures came the flies. There were millions of them buzzing all over the stronghold like a plague of desert locusts.

The beleaguered inhabitants of the stronghold tried everything, including quicklime and flame-throwers, to get rid of the bodies. Nothing worked.

Quite soon the men began to fall sick, exhibiting symptoms ranging from flatulence to anorexia, vomiting, dysentery, heartburn, muscle cramps and severe depression.

These, added to a sudden outbreak of malaria, notably among the white sojas, and trench foot, several cases of typhoid and a mysterious condition characterised by a burning, tingling and itching sensation all over the limbs, soon reduced White City into nothing more than a sickward. Many more Chindits than were killed by the Japs would later die from these illnesses after they were evacuated. The brass in India didn't much care for them, but they didn't exactly hate them either. More medics were flown in. Dozens of parachutes carrying cargoes of medication descended on the block.

But what everyone wanted, more than anything else, was to get out of White City. They wanted out of the putrid stench in the block, but not necessarily out of Burma. Few felt inclined to leave until the job they'd been sent to do in Burma was done, and that job would not be done until the last Japanese soja had been kicked out of Burma.

Every assignment that sent the sojas out of the block was now considered a luxury.

There were only two assignments out of the block that were conceivable in the jungle. The first, which was dangerous but relatively easy going, was to go outside the main block to fetch drinking water from a nearby ford.

The second – the most dangerous for a Chindit – was to be sent out floating: to blow up bridges or to lay an ambuscade. More floating Chindits died at the hands of the Japs or were consumed by the jungle than were killed by the coal scuttle in any of the strongholds.

Being sent floating was once considered bad news. Now

everyone wanted to go. This was why D-Section jumped for joy when Kyaftin Gillafsie told them they were to go with him to Maiganga. Even Guntu, whose fear of trees and shadow-abductors was as fresh as ever, reacted with something like celebration. He still looked very sad but he did a double somersault.

The only reason Bloken didn't go with them was because he had been down with severe diarrhoea and was so weak he couldn't even climb out of the trench unaided.

11

Bloken was in tears when D-Section left White City without him. As he cried, the sunbeams slipping into the trench bounced off his newly acquired gold teeth – spoils of war freshly harvested from the mouths of dead Japs – and lit up the walls around him.

Bloken blamed his amulets for failing him. He now realised the charms had let him down because when he acquired them in Gboko, his home town in Tivland, he had gone to the snake-oil pedlar instead of going to the Great Priest whose charms cost a whopping sixpence more. It wasn't because Bloken was a miser; on the day he bought the charms he'd been drunk on sweet palm wine, and on a potent home-brewed gin which was called Push-Me-I-Push-You because a man drunk on it entered a dizzying state in which he thought he was walking forward and backward and upward and downward and to the left and to the right all at the same time when in fact he was simply swaying in one spot.

He'd had several gallons of Burukutu, a vinegary malt beer made from fermented millet.

Then he'd moved on to Pito, a glorious chaser which was no chaser at all. Pito, like the wonderful Burukutu, was a hallucinogenic cider made from maize and millet but fermented for only half the time.

He'd topped up by smoking wee-wee, a fragrant, medicinal herb derived from the dried flowers of top-grade, non-industrial Gboko hemp.

It was a mind-bending cocktail which always had the curious effect of making Bloken break bottles on his bald head just to show how tough he was.

To spice things up, he had a girl on each arm. They were two beautiful angels called Patience and Angerina. Patience and Angerina said they were sisters but he knew they were only teasing him. But – to tell the truth – he wouldn't be surprised if they were sisters because each sister looked just as beautiful as the other. He couldn't honestly remember where he'd picked them up. But they were the most beautiful angels he'd picked up who were not sisters since the last beautiful sisters who were also angels he'd picked up in bars whose names and locations he couldn't quite remember probably because the bars didn't really exist. Beautiful angels and angelic sisters simply gravitated towards the magnetic fields of the money in his pouch. He couldn't ask anything more of life.

Bloken was so spaced out he could barely walk, but

Patience and Angerina had fallen madly in love with him, which was a wonderful thing because Bloken was also head over heels in love with them. Between the two of them, the sisters half-carried, half-dragged him to where they thought he said he wanted to go. The three of them sang heartily all the way there. The girls gasped and stopped singing when they heard Bloken sing. They told him he had the most beautiful singing voice they'd ever heard. This was no mean praise. Everyone in Gboko had a beautiful voice. Everyone in Gboko was a wonderful singer. Gboko children came out of the womb crying in perfect pitch.

Unfortunately for Bloken, the beautiful sisters were so enchanted by his beautiful voice they took a wrong turning and dragged him to the wrong place.

His fate was sealed from that moment.

Bloken was a good boy really, a hard-working farmer-boy. He'd been out on the town only because it was his last New Yam festival. It was the day before he laid down his hoe and joined thousands of other Tiv boys who had been specially invited by the District Officer, who said the Tiv were a martial race, a race of great warriors, to come to his office on the first market day after the New Yam festival to take the king's shilling. Never mind the king's shilling, what Bloken really wanted was to go to blaady fackin India. He didn't give a fack what he had to go and do in blaady fackin Boma just so long as he got to go to the wonderful fackin India he'd heard so much about.

Bloken loved swange music. In particular he loved the

swange music of Louis Armstrong, Benny Goodman and Fletcher Henderson. He hoped they had swange music in India.

But Bloken was no fool. He knew he couldn't take any chances against those Japs he was sure to be facing in Boma. This was why he decided to bullet-proof himself before heading out to fight for the king.

Unfortunately for him, he got totally wasted on the day he chose to carry out this mission, and through no fault of their own Patience and Angerina, the loves of his life, took him to the wrong bullet-proof salesman.

The snake-oil man took Bloken's hard-earned money and gave him a string of beads filled with nothing but sand scooped up from the banks of the river Katsina-Ala.

It was these sham amulets, Bloken decided, which had given him the runs when he should have been out there heading for Maiganga. It was the greatest disappointment in Bloken's life, but he was only eighteen and every latest disappointment was the greatest disappointment in his life.

Bloken Yahimba was saved by the greatest disappointment in his life.

12

Ko Ye walked into the booby trap at sunset.

The march had been easier than they'd thought it would be. Most of it had happened along a gentle slope winding through a jungle that was not terrifying so much as it was breathtakingly humbling.

They went through forests of tall, lean neem trees, and tall, fat oak and jati trees. They beheld an endless spectacle of flamboyant Gulmohar trees whose long golden branches bloomed with feathery emerald leaves and bright orange-red flowers. They came across mango trees and feasted on the ripe, succulent fruit that came raining to the ground when they caught hold of the branches and shook them.

A python came slithering down with the mangoes. Guntu, who had seen many snakes on mango trees in his time, despatched it with one swipe of his *adda*.

When the march resumed, Danja and Banana, who were now at the back, greedily bit into their mangoes. and talked about the letter from Samanja Pash. The samanja had written to D-Section from his hospital bed in Calcutta where he was recovering after the amputation.

'So now he has a wooden leg?' Banana asked. He'd been on sentry duty the night the letter arrived.

'Not yet,' replied Danja. 'They have to wait for the wound from the cut to heal before they give him a wooden leg.'

'It's hard to think of Pash with a wooden leg.'

'I'd rather have a wooden leg than end up like Dogo – God rest him. Pash is a lucky man. They're even sending him back home next month. On a boat going to Laagos.'

'Is he from Laagos?'

'He's from Abbeykutey.'

'Where is that?'

'Not far from Laagos.'

'Will he be going back to his old job with the railways in Minna?'

'Who knows?'

'Pity about his father. Was it a cobra?'

'No. I don't think so.'

'Such a terrible way to go.'

'I think it was a carpet viper.'

'Ouch. Ouch. Ouch. Why didn't they tell Samanja Pash?'

'The kyaftin says the wire got lost in India. By the time it arrived here, Pash was already in Calcutta.'

'So he still doesn't know about it?'

'I don't think so. Any letters from home lately?'

'Not for me. What about you?'

'None for me either,' said Danja. 'Guntu got one a few weeks ago. His brother wrote to tell him that his wife's just had twins.'

'Guntu's wife has had twins?'

'Two fine little sojas.'

'God is great.'

'The poor woman was pregnant for fifteen months.'

'I didn't know that was possible,' Banana said.

'Neither did I,' said Danja. 'It's a miracle.'

'I wonder why Guntu's kept so quiet about it,' said Banana.

'I think it's because he's a bit embarrassed.'

'What's there to be embarrassed about?'

'You know Guntu. He's a modest man. He doesn't want anyone thinking there's anything special about him.'

'I would be happy if such a thing were to happen to me. I would run up to everyone I knew and tell them about it.'

'I'm sure you would,' said Danja. 'Let me ask you a question, Ali. Don't be embarrassed. Have you ever slept with a woman?'

Banana blushed and giggled.

'That's a serious matter,' Danja declared. 'We must do something about it as soon as we get back to India. Bloken found a place in Bombay during the week we spent there. He kept going back every night. I went once with him. Well, twice. It was glorious, Ali. You'll like it. I went back three times.'

'Make up your mind. How many times did you go there?'

'Every single night. Let me tell you about those girls in Bombay, Ali –'

'I thought you were married.'

'I am. By the grace of God I am. What has my wife got to do with any of this?'

'"Do not even go near fornication." That's what it says in the Great Book.'

'You sound just like the samanja. That's exactly what he said to me back in Bombay. He thinks he knows about life, but he doesn't. He only knows about killing. How well do you know the Great Book?'

'Well enough.'

'Then you'll appreciate these great words which the prophet himself addressed to us miserable sons of Adam, "And whatever you have been given is an enjoyment of the life of this world and its finery."'

'That's not all of it.'

'You're right. There's a lot more than that in the Holy Book.'

'"And that which is with God is better and will remain for ever. Have you then no sense?" That's what it says at the end of that verse.'

'I was just about to come to that part,' said Danja. 'Wonderful words. Words of wisdom.'

'And it says nothing about fornication.'

'That is quite true. But I'm going to take you to those girls when we get to Bombay even if I have to drag you there. I'll even pay from my own pocket.'

'Why does it matter to you so much?' Banana asked.

'It matters to me,' said Danja suddenly furious, 'because life is a cruel joker, Ali. One moment we're here, the next moment we're not. We must live it to the full. Do you really think Guntu's wife carried those twins in her womb for a year and three months? You really think it's Japs turning into shadows and trees that's made him lose his mind? Innocence is a dangerous virtue, Ali, and I'll rid you of it even if I end up in the fires of all the seven hells one right after the other. Don't get me wrong, you're a brave soja, a fine fighter. But killing men does not make a man of you. I'll make a man of you, Ali. I'll lead you astray, if God gives me the strength.'

Banana sniggered.

'I will, I will, mark my words, I will,' said Danja, jabbing Banana in the neck with his finger. 'You may not thank me for it, but I'm not doing it for gratitude. I'm a fisherman, Ali. I can tell you one or two things about the perils of innocence. A raging stream will forgive you for being stupid, but it will not forgive you for being innocent. An innocent fisherman is a dead fisherman. If it's the will of God, my brother, you and I will taste the pleasures of Bombay. Virginity is a curable illness. Let the sin be on my head.'

Their path was littered with yew trees, chestnuts, yellow-throated blue-violet daisies, crimson-purple rhododendrons, white magnolias, slipper orchids, yellow dog-roses, blue poppies, wild cherries, red lilies, flowering dogwood, cobalt-blue stemless gentians, coffin-trees, musk plants, moss hills, and the dazzling but foul-smelling sundew flower which enticed mosquitoes, gnats, spiders, butter-flies, crickets and grasshoppers onto its leaves with a glowing, sticky liquid, a digestive sap which dissolved their bodies once the spoon-shaped leaves suddenly snapped shut on them, trapping them inside and turning into their funeral urn.

They saw a clouded leopard dragging a barking deer up a large, sprawling Bo tree.

They saw an entire forest of cypress trees that had been almost completely wiped out of existence by strangler figs – a proud member of the freeloading banyan tribe which usually started life as a harmless seed at the foot or on top of another tree before slowly sprouting roots of its own and growing into a tight mesh around the trunk of its hapless host, strangling it piecemeal, depriving it of sunlight, snatching all nourishment from its roots until it shrivelled and died, leaving a hollow in the strangler's trunk where the tree it murdered had stood for generations. The strangler fig was the prince of parasites.

Early in the afternoon, a wild elephant appeared along their path daring them to come and move her. They bowed to her majesty and changed their course.

They were less than three kilometres from their destin-ation when they walked into the ambush. To the west, the sky appeared to be on fire. Its flames rapidly changed from a golden saffron tint to a purple cast of brown; from violet quartz it sank into the dark blue of night.

Ahead of them lay a stream.

'With any luck,' said Ko to Guntu behind him, 'we should be in Nyaunggaing in an hour's time.'

191

Those were his last words. They were also the last words Guntu ever heard.

Ko carefully stepped across a suspect looking bamboo stem which lay across his path. He avoided it because he thought it looked like a booby trap. He was about to turn round to warn the others when he felt a soft, almost imperceptible resistance to his foot. He looked down and realised his foot was caught under what was clearly the trip wire of a mine. As he suddenly froze in his tracks, Guntu bumped into him and seconds later several luminous metallic fruits dropped out of the trees above, much like the mangoes that had earlier rained on them, and exploded into a dense constellation of rattling bullets.

Ko Ye and Guntu never stood a chance. They died instantly.

The other Chindits barely had time to recover from the numbing shock when the heart-stopping and very familiar barks of Nambu machine guns and the crack of Arisaka bolt-action rifles broke out around them.

Banana stood rooted to the spot, absolutely petrified, slow to understand what was happening to them. Through the corner of his eye, he saw Danja and Gillafsie reel and topple over as they were hit. Damisa and Godiwillin were nowhere to be seen.

Then something struck him in the chest. He thought it was a bullet, but it wasn't. It was a punch from Damisa, and he found himself flying headlong and dazed into the stream below.

Streams and the planet Mars were roughly the same distance from Banana until he became a Chindit, when he found during training that he took easily to water. But it hadn't quite sunk into him during those months in India that he would one day find himself trying to hold his breath under water while bullets and grenades were exploding just above his head. He quickly came to his limit of endurance and began quite involuntarily to rise to the surface.

Just before his head emerged from the water, he felt something grab hold of his foot and drag him back into the depths. He gasped for air and swallowed several pints of warm, brackish water.

He felt like throwing up. He threw up and swallowed more water. He thrashed violently trying to break away, but Damisa's grip was firm and even with only one hand free he was swimming away with long powerful strokes toward the northern bank of the stream. Banana swung around and tried to bite him, every fibre in his body gripped by panic, every part of him screaming with terror.

The last thing Banana heard before his body went limp and the lights in his head dimmed were the dull reports of the machine guns.

13

Banana woke to crashes of thunder.

His eyes blinked open and snapped shut again as the jungle lit up with streaks of lightning rising like a blazing wall of pikes from the forest floor and colliding just above the trees with the great flashes of light coming from the angry sky.

The sheets of rain which now poured down on him tore into his body like cowhide switches. In the brief interludes of fierce lightning and the thick blanket of darkness that swaddled him, he caught burnt-out glimpses of the lifeless shape of a man stretched out on the grass beside him.

Damisa was dead.

Holding his breath, Banana prodded him with his elbow. Damisa did not respond. Banana prodded him again.

Damisa stirred. His hand rose weakly and then buckled back to his side.

He was alive. Damisa was alive.

Such was the sheer intensity of Banana's relief that he forgot the torrential downpour. He forgot his terror of the trees swaying like drunken evil spirits everywhere he looked. He forgot the roaring forest around him and the fearsome beasts prowling in the dark. He sat there in a crouch, rocking back and forth, vaguely wondering where he was, how he got there and what had happened to Damisa.

The rain poured all night long. It stopped briefly at daybreak and then returned as a gentle, steady shower.

14

Damisa was in a truly bad way. When Banana tried to move him, he yelled in pain. He could talk quite clearly and, except for the blood that kept coming up when he coughed, it was difficult to see what was wrong with him. Obviously in great pain, he told Banana what happened while Banana was unconscious the night before.

Fortunately, he said, they had reached the north bank when Banana passed out. Damisa carried him out of the water. The Japs were still enfilading the stream. Bullets whizzed behind them and sank like rain droplets into the water. Under the dark, starless night, brewing with the storms of the coming monsoon, he struggled to resuscitate the farabiti. It was after he'd succeeded and was getting to his feet, with Banana in his arms, to move further away from the bank when he felt something sharp strike him in the back.

It was a bullet lodging itself just below his heart.

15

'You'll have to go on alone,' Damisa said tonelessly. 'It's over for me.'

There was no self-pity in his voice. His face was already settling into the ashen mask of death.

'Maiganga isn't far off,' said Banana. 'If we can get to Maiganga, the commander there can radio for help.'

'They were expecting us last night,' Damisa told him. 'The mission they wanted us for was to take place this morning. Kyaftin Gillafsie didn't say what the mission was. But they would have left Maiganga already. Don't go to Maiganga. Head back to the stronghold.'

'I think Will also escaped the Japs last night,' Banana said. 'He couldn't have gone far in that rain. I didn't see him come into the water. I think he's still somewhere on the south bank. If I can find him, the two of us can carry you back.'

'You don't understand, Ali. There's nothing that can be done for me now, even if this had happened inside the stronghold,' Damisa said, his eyes shut. 'Will didn't escape. I saw him go down. He was the first to be hit after Guntu and Ko were blown up. He caught it straight between the eyes. Will is dead, Ali, and I'll soon be on my way too. You're the only one left. Go back to the stronghold and tell them what happened to us.'

'I'm not leaving here without you, Samanja. I can't do that.'

'Can you find your way back to White City?' Damisa asked, ignoring what Banana had just said.

'I can. We both can.'

'Don't go anywhere near the place we were ambushed. There might still be mines there. Walk along the river further east and find a safe place to cross onto the south bank. The river is always treacherous after a heavy rain. Be careful you don't get swept away. When you've crossed, head back west and then find a way to get back on the route that brought us here. Don't go anywhere near the scene of the ambush. Head six o'clock for about five miles and when you reach the killer figs it's three o'clock again from there and straight on to the stronghold.'

'We're going back together, Samanja. I'm not leaving you here.'

Damisa laughed weakly, mirthlessly. 'I can't move, Ali. And you'll only kill me if you tried to move me. You're talking to a dead man, my friend.' His body shook with more coughing and he spat out more blood. 'You must call on my wife if you ever go to Kano. Her name is Hasana. She has a stall at Kurmi market where she sells spices. There's a pair of earrings in my rucksack. I bought them for her in India. Tell her my death was quick and that I suffered no pain.'

'I can't leave you here, Samanja,' Banana said, beginning to get desperate.

'If you stay here, you'll die as well,' Damisa told him. 'You don't need to be a shehu to know that there are Japs living somewhere in this neck of the woods. Sooner or later, one of their patrols is bound to come here. What good will it do the two of us if we both died when one of us could have lived? You have to go on on your own but I'm not asking you to leave me here.'

'What do you mean?' Banana asked suspiciously although he knew exactly what Damisa meant.

'You know what I mean, Ali,' said Damisa. 'You know what the Japs do when they come upon our wounded. They cut off their limbs and rip open their stomachs. It's either Jap or the leopards and tigers if you leave me here.'

'My ammo is all soaked,' Banana said disconsolately. 'And I lost my rucksack during the ambush so —'

Damisa cut him short.

'As you can see, I've still got mine,' he said. He'd tied it by the strap to his hand after he was shot. 'I've got two revolvers in a plastic pouch in there and they're both loaded.'

Banana did not move.

200

'I'd do it myself if I had the strength,' said Damisa, beginning to plead. 'It's the only thing you can do for me, Ali, nothing more.'

Banana opened the rucksack and found the plastic pouch. He pulled out an Enfield revolver and a Browning P-35 Hi-Power. He returned the Enfield into the pouch and dejectedly eyed the P-35.

'Bring out the blanket,' said Damisa. 'Use it to muffle the sound. There may be Jap nearby.'

Banana reached into the rucksack and pulled out a blanket.

'Thank you, Ali,' said Damisa. 'I know this isn't easy for you, but you can't even begin to imagine the pain I'm in. It's a shame but that's life. But I've had a really good life too, you know, and so many good friends. And I'll never forget my brothers in D-Section. And the kyaftin too, he was a good sort.' He shivered. 'It's cold out. I'm ready when you are.'

Damisa shut his eyes and patiently waited for death.

Banana checked the pistol's double-stack magazine to confirm that it was loaded.

'Goodbye, Samanja,' he said.

Damisa said nothing.

'Thank you for saving my life,' he said.

Damisa said nothing.

'Till we meet again,' he said.

But Damisa still did not respond. It was as if he was already dead.

Carefully Banana laid the folded blanket on Damisa's forehead.

Carefully he placed the muzzle of the gun on the blanket.

'I'm about to do it,' he said and waited for Damisa to say something. But Damisa did not respond.

'I'm about to do it, Samanja,' Banana called out again, like a delinquent child begging to be stopped from carrying out his wayward intention.

His hands were shaking.

'Speak to me, Samanja,' he begged, the tears streaming down his face. 'Don't ignore me. Don't ignore me, please.'

'Get a grip on yourself, Banana,' Damisa said hoarsely. 'Do it now.'

Banana wiped the tears off his cheeks and pulled the trigger.

A flock of brown dippers sunbathing on a rock nearby screeched in alarm and dived to the bottom of the water where they stayed for a whole minute. When they emerged from the belly of the stream they had established a healthier distance between themselves and the frightening sound. A curious wild dog that had been watching the two men all morning growled angrily and scampered off.

Banana knelt by Damisa's body for a long while.

He wrapped Damisa in the blanket he'd used to muffle the gun. He found a rope in the rucksack and tied it round Damisa's feet, round his neck and round his thighs.

He picked up the rucksack and strapped it to his back.

He knelt down and lifted the body. Damisa, a towering giant of a man, was light as a suckling.

At the edge of the stream, Banana stopped and said a

prayer over Damisa's body. Then he eased Damisa onto the swollen waters.

He watched the body slowly drift away on the westward tide.

He walked away in the other direction, turning every so often to glance back at Damisa. He stopped looking only after the body disappeared around a bend in the river.

16

Banana's journey back to White City was painfully slow. It wasn't simply because he was totally exhausted, or just because the trek back was uphill all the way. Overnight the jungle had turned into a giant bed of sludge. When he wasn't up to his waist in mud, the path was so slippery he repeatedly landed with his face in the mush.

He walked all day in the heavy rain.

He reached the strangler figs at night and made camp there. He opened a can of bully-beef and made a quick meal of it without bothering to heat it although the rain had stopped and he could easily have made a fire. But he knew that making a fire at night was asking for trouble if there happened to be enemy traffic passing.

Damisa appeared just as he was taking his Mepacrine and getting ready to retire for the night. Banana tried talking to him but the samanja simply stood there smiling at him and saying nothing.

Banana climbed into his trench. He pulled the thatched log roof he'd made over the hole and fell asleep almost immediately. He was awakened barely an hour later by howling winds and frenetic lightning and thunder. Within minutes of the rain starting again, his trench had become a well of water.

He heard trees crashing all around him. It didn't bother him one bit. He saw lightning strike a tree close by, ripping it apart. He could no longer be bothered to worry. He felt nothing but contempt for death.

He flung the rucksack into the hollow trunk of a fig tree. A startled snake scrambled out of the tree and slithered away. Banana climbed into the hollow, rested his head on the rucksack and curled up. The magnificent parasite tree swayed a few times in the relentless storm and at one point during the night while Banana was asleep when he thought he was fully awake, he felt he was at sea on a ship taking him back home. King George appeared dressed as the emir of Zaria. For no apparent reason, Banana found this unbelievably funny and burst out laughing.

He was still laughing when he woke up in the morning. He realised that the deep panic that had taken hold of him since a week before he flew into Burma had suddenly evaporated.

He suspected that it had something to do with Damisa's death. Damisa's death had been unlike any other.

Banana had now killed many men in his time and he'd seen many men die. The men he'd killed had been faceless. He didn't know them and didn't hate them. He felt nothing about killing them. They would have done the same to him. He was a foot soldier fighting a crazy war he didn't even really understand. He didn't understand why King George was waging a war in Burma from far away England. And it didn't matter to him.

He was in Burma to fight King George's war and that was the end of the matter.

The Japs were King George's enemies and that was the end of the matter.

The Japs were his enemies.

He would kill the Japs or the Japs would kill him.

That was the end of the matter.

It was a different matter though with the men around him whose deaths he'd witnessed. They were all men he'd come to know very well. They were all men who'd become closer to him than any member of his own family had ever been. These men were his brothers and he'd watched them die one after the other. He'd had no time to mourn them and he couldn't say what he'd learnt from their deaths except that next time it might be his turn. And that had been a terrifying thought.

The thought of death had been the most terrifying thing weighing on his mind but Damisa's death had changed that.

Now the thought of death filled him with scorn.

I laugh at you, he said to death. I laugh at you.

When he woke up in the morning, the rain had stopped. The sky was aglow with the sun.

Banana picked up his rucksack and stepped out of the tree trunk. He headed due west, singing out loud.

He walked all day filled with a rising sense of exhilaration that made him want to dance. So he stopped and danced, watched by an audience of bemused monkeys. The monkeys booed at him.

At sunset he arrived at an area in the jungle that looked very familiar to him. He wondered if he was close to White City. But he knew it couldn't be. He sniffed the air. It was too clean. There wasn't the stench of death anywhere here.

As he stood wondering where on earth this might be, a snake slid out of the hollow trunk of a tree and slithered away. He realised what he had done. He'd gone round full circle and arrived exactly where he'd set out from that morning.

He was grateful to the snake.

'Come back, my friend,' he called after it. 'There's room enough for both of us. It's your home after all. There's room enough for every one of us.'

But the snake didn't return.

He made a fire. He brought out his meal pack, the last one he had, and emptied the bully-beef, the fruit bar, the biscuits, the grape sugar, the lemonade powder and the tea into the kettle. He added some water to it, stirred it all together and brought it to the boil.

It was the best meal he'd had since he came to Burma.

He was so excited about his culinary discovery he wanted to run to the D-Section dugout and tell all the boys. He had to restrain himself because he thought it might be too dangerous this time of night. The coal scuttles would soon arrive.

After the meal, he lit up a Chesterfield and luxuriated in the splendour of his surroundings.

He did not bother digging a trench that night. He threw the rucksack into the hollow and crept in after it.

It rained all through the night but he didn't once wake up.

He got up in the morning to find himself covered in leeches. He pulled off his uniform, his underpants, his boots and his socks. Stark naked, he looked at himself and found thousands of tiny, slug-like creatures clinging to his body, from his head to his toes, sucking his blood.

He started pulling them out, but then he saw that once they'd had their fill, once their famished little bodies had swollen up with his blood, the leeches simply retracted their muscular, needle-sharp, flesh-puncturing snouts from his body and fell to the ground in a happy swoon. He could tell they were happy because the blood-sucking worms, each blessed with three saw-like jaws armed with a hundred razor-sharp teeth and with stomachs big enough to hold blood up to five times their body size, broke into dance immediately they came out of the swoon. There was no doubt in Banana's mind that the joyous, up-and-down acrobatics into which their bodies rose and fell, and which gave them the appearance of swimming while standing still, was a dance of ecstasy and gratitude.

'Help yourselves to it, my friends,' Banana said to the blood-suckers. 'There's a lot more where that came from.'

They were his guests, after all. It would be rude of him not to offer them a meal.

He stuffed his uniform, his boots, his underpants and his socks into the rucksack and was about to slip his hands through the straps to hoist it on his back when he realised that it might crush the poor little creatures feeding behind his chest.

He apologised profusely to the leeches and flung the rucksack back into the tree trunk. He pushed his rifle into the hollow and hurled his *adda* away.

'I'm sorry to have broken into your lovely home two nights in a row,' he said in a loud voice, hoping the generous snake was nearby and listening to him. 'As a token of my gratitude, I've left a bag in your backyard. In the bag you'll find two pistols, a Bren rifle, some ammunition and quite a few grenades. You'll find many other things in it. You're welcome to them all. I would have gifted you with a stallion to go with the guns, but the only horse I've ever had turned out not to be a horse at all. It was in fact a donkey, and it is no longer of this world. It would have given me great pleasure to see you, my gallant friend, perched on a horse and with a rifle in your hands. Did I mention the pistols? There's a Browning and an Enfield. They're yours now. They both belonged to the samanja. But the samanja's dead so he won't need them.'

17

Unarmed, and without so much as a table knife on him, and naked as the day he was born, Ali Banana made his journey across the jungle.

Ai remembah when ai was a soja,
Ai remembah when ai was a soja,
Ai remembah when ai was a soja,
Ai remembah when ai was a soja.

Hippee ya ya hippee hippee ya-ya,
Hippee ya ya hippee hippee ya-ya,
Hippee ya ya hippee hippee ya-ya,
Hippee ya ya hippee hippee ya-ya.

He was still singing when he finally made it back to the stronghold three days later.

He'd survived on a diet of leeches.

The sentries took one look at the naked African singing loudly as he approached the wire and rushed to help him inside. His face was badly swollen and covered in leech bites. They couldn't make out who he was but they knew that any black man in Burma had to be one of them. All they could tell was that the man looked to be about fifty years old.

Banana was deliriously happy to see the Chindits and except for the thousand tiny Y-shaped bruises on his body, and the several dozen freshly acquired leeches still feasting on him, they couldn't work out what was wrong with him.

He was all smiles until they offered him a blanket to cover his nakedness.

'The Janar,' he declared, 'would spit on your blanket.'

So he spat on it in the name of the Janar.

They led him straight to Brigade HQ.

He got quite irate when the Brigade Commander offered him a seat.

'Can't you see I've got guests?' he yelled at the commander wagging a rebuking finger at the officer. 'Can't you see they'll die if I sat on them?'

He pulled out a particularly well-nourished leech stuck to his thigh and flung it into his mouth.

'They said I could eat them,' he explained as he crunched the worm between his teeth. 'They didn't want me to die.'

Samanja Show, who had heard about the naked African visitor, came in as Banana was helping himself to another blood-filled delicacy and immediately turned round and went out again. He was heard throwing up outside the bunker.

When the commander asked after his health, Banana mumbled something about a snake.

'She was so kind to me,' he said shaking his head in wonder. 'I would have given her a stallion if I had one to give away. Where's Bloken?'

The telephone wires and walkie-talkies in White City went crazy for Bloken.

Bloken, who looked like a spirit, having shat out everything he ate and lost more than half his body weight, reported to HQ feverish and slightly light-headed.

Banana was overjoyed to see him.

'Bloken!' he trilled. 'I'm so glad to see you, Bloken, my brother. I'd give you a big hug, but I can't, you see, my friends are having supper.'

Bloken's jaw fell wide open. He stared groggily at the mad man talking to him.

'Who are you?' he asked, genuinely bewildered. He'd never seen this man before.

'Bloken, it's me,' Banana gushed, his voice full of love. 'It's me, Ali Banana. It's so good to see you, Bloken.'

Bloken burst into tears.

Kurunkus kan dan bera.

That is all.
Off with the rat's head.

Author's Note

I am gratefully indebted to the late Sergeant James Shaw – who makes a cameo appearance in this novel under the guise of the fictional Samanja Jamees Show – whose unforgettable account of his Chindit experience, *The March Out*, introduced me to the real-life Ali Banana (whose imaginary namesake is pure invention and bears no resemblance whatsoever to his historical forerunner). Captain Charles Carfrae's *Chindit Column* proved similarly invaluable. These books together with Brigadier Michael 'Mad Mike' Calvert's classic war memoir, *Prisoners of Hope*, first-hand accounts of the Chindits, all chronicle salutary instances of the courage and resourcefulness shown by the Africans who served with them in Burma, and enabled me in no small way to rediscover that searingly vivid and yet dizzyingly phantasmagoric world of the jungles of mainland South East Asia into which my father's stories of carnage, shell-shock and hard-won compassion first immersed me when I was little more than an infant.

I wish to thank the Imperial War Museum where I spent many afternoons delving into declassified military files about the Second World War and its least documented and most brutal theatre, the Burma Campaign.

I would like to acknowledge my debt also to the following books: *Orde Wingate* by Christopher Sykes; *Orde Wingate: Irregular Soldier* by Trevor Royle; *Fire in the Night* by John Bierman and Colin Smith; *War Bush* by John A. L. Hamilton; *West Africans at War* by Peter Clarke. I have borrowed quite liberally from a true story entitled *The Last Public Execution in Sokoto Prison* published in the anthology *A Selection of Hausa Stories* compiled by H.A.S Johnston. I owe a world of gratitude to all of these sources.

I would also like to thank all those friends and family members who pointed me in the right direction and who supported me when I was writing this book: Temi T. and Andrea; Ona, Rana and Keith; Nick Rankin; Johanna Ekström; Charles Taylor; and my editor, Ellah Allfrey, who encouraged me to write this book and who made it a better one. I would also like to thank the Arts Council England for the grant which allowed me to work on this novel.

Biyi Bandele
London